I0607911

Dead To Life

Dead To Life

Also by R. L. Rhyse

The Margaret of Greenwich® Series

R. L. Rhyse

Dead To Life

Wyston Books, Inc.

Dead To Life

Wyston Books, Inc.
www.wystonbooks.com

Dead To Life: a novel

ISBN: 978-1-7376816-5-6
eISBN: 978-1-7376816-4-9

Cover Photograph by CasarsaGuru
Licensed From Getty Images

BISAC: FIC 043000 FICTION/Coming of Age
FIC 050000 FICTION/Crime

"When the perishable has been clothed with the imperishable, and the mortal with immortality, then the saying that is written will come true: Death has been swallowed up in victory."

1 Corinthians 15:54-55

"And ye shall know the truth and the truth shall make you free."

John 8:32

"In the depth of winter I finally learned that within me there lay an invincible summer."

Albert Camus

Dead To Life

Introduction

It took the strenuous efforts of an expensive lawyer to permit me to bid farewell to my father. Which would all have been unnecessary had I not been fourteen. But long-held prison rules are loathe to change, "flexible" not being part of their vocabulary especially when public reaction is feared. Like with so many matters, politics rules the day.

Yet how could anyone object to a teenager speaking to her loving father particularly when her long absent mother had been publicized as an alcoholic whore? I couldn't imagine as I fainted, while our car exited the prison's gate.

Chapter 1

My psychoanalyst didn't take insurance or credit cards. During our last session each month he would hand me a bill itemizing my fee, which was the number of sessions he treated me that month times five-hundred-dollars. He wasn't cheap as his statement to my husband indicated. "My great-grandfather was Anna Freud's internist," Doctor Hess had told him. It was a good line, my husband bought it, and I became Doctor Hess' patient three mornings a week, sitting up and talking face-to-face. Having been molested at sixteen, there would be no laying down on the couch for me you understand.

"What are you thinking?" Doctor Hess had asked me on a blustery winter day two-years later.

I had been hesitant to state this even though, with an analyst, speaking freely is a cardinal rule of treatment.

"That nothing seems to be happening. I'm not making more changes except for becoming pregnant. Which has nothing to do with you," I said, in an attempt at humor.

"Maybe..." he said.

For a therapy patient to deny that *any* positive life event is unrelated to her treatment seems to wound their doctor's narcissism, like telling a mother that her baby is ugly.

But his reaction surprised me.

"I agree. Your nightmares have gone, and you've become orgasmic. You didn't even flinch when your hand accidentally brushed mine yesterday," he said with a small smile.

I also smiled, but to indicate recognition of his jest. Men get depressed when you don't consider their joke funny.

I said nothing, sensing more was coming.

"I think you should write a book about your life. Your college newspaper printed three of your essays so you must be a talented writer. Considering your experiences a literary agent would hunger for you as a client."

"You're *serious*?" I asked, unbelievingly.

"As serious as life," he said, yielding another smile.

"Telling the truth about what happened could get me killed," I said, after some thinking.

"You needn't tell *everything*. You could decide what to leave out, and the events happened years ago. All principals are locked away in a super-max or dead."

"That's true," I said.

"Think about it. It might be what you need to gain the emotional freedom you deserve. You have a baby to think about too."

So I did.

Brian, my husband, made it a practice to never ask how my therapy went. "If your wife tells you what she speaks of during her treatment she won't speak freely to me," Doctor Hess warned Brian when my treatment began. But I must have looked different that evening.

"You looked pleased when you came home," he mused.

"Yes, I've decided on a new project. I'm going to write a book.

Chapter 2

Seated before my laptop, I considered how to write a book. Should I start typing and not stop until it's completed? No, this would lead to madness and the destruction of my marriage too. So I vowed to write six-hundred words (about two typed pages) daily before stopping. By following this schedule I could continue being supportive to my husband, who labored mightily as a fellow lawyer.

But I'm getting ahead of my story. Maybe because it concerns the safe and comfortable part, the one that won't get us killed. Or is this unrealistic since what Doctor Hess said was true: most of the principals in my story are dead or in a supermax. And would anyone really care so long after my father's execution?

My thinking returned to childhood which, it has been said, is a writer's bank balance. All that money could buy had enveloped my early years though not warmth or emotion. These *were* happy I then thought for no child can tolerate believing otherwise.

Enough for my first day's writing, I told myself, closing my laptop as Brian entered our bedroom. Being a habitual person, he parked his Glock on the night table at his side of the bed before kissing me. My Glock was on the other.

Chapter 3

When my daughter's life began, at her conception that is, I didn't feel different right away. Which isn't unusual, I was told. The early signs of pregnancy occur in some women a week or two after conception with others noticing nothing until their period is noticeably late. A woman's reactions are individual and, though always feeling myself different, I now seemed to have joined the flock.

Having always been a good student, I excitedly joined the hospital's "First Mother's" class taught by a nurse-practitioner and mother of four. "She should know!" the seatmate beside me remarked and I nodded absently.

Reaching for the pad and pen in my bag, I began feeling hot. "I'm sick," I told myself before my analyst's reassuring advice took hold. "Anxiety can mimic *any* medical symptom. Many who fear they're having a heart attack and rush to the Emergency Room are only suffering a panic attack which is when the normal symptoms of anxiety are misinterpreted as a deadly medical event. When the fear happens, tell yourself you're healthy, experiencing the normal symptoms of anxiety and it'll disappear."

I did and it did as our instructor began.

"Because growing a new life is awe-inspiring and exciting, it will be normal for you to feel vulnerable and anxious. Added to this are the big changes happening in your body: higher hormonal levels of progesterone and estrogen often cause unwanted side effects like feeling tired and sick, having mood swings or being easily irritated."

"Sounds like my husband," a woman called out and everyone laughed.

"Right!" said the instructor and continued.

"You may also have unsettling thoughts: that you might accidentally eat or drink something which will harm your baby, wonder if you can continue having sex or what giving birth will be like. Perhaps most of all, whether you will be a good parent especially if your parents weren't."

Heads nodded and I wondered what the reaction would be were I to reveal that my father was an executed murderer and my mother an alcoholic whore.

Chapter 4

What and when I did learn about my parents are questions I've often asked myself. Which is inevitable considering who they were. Did I sense my father being a killer-for-hire and my mother having lovers early, facts which I'd feared to think? No child could tolerate believing these. My years of treatment with Doctor Hess had always led me to the same conclusion: that I hadn't known.

My father, Giovanni (we called him "Joe") had been an ideal father. When not away "on business" he attended all my school functions and parent-teacher meetings. "You're the smartest student and your teachers love you!" he would tell me. Then, with a beaming smile, I would accept his gift of a hundred-dollar bill for my piggy bank. He eventually took me to the bank where it was deposited as the beginning of my college fund. I would become the first college graduate in our large extended family.

Joe was a much liked always smiling neighbor. Spontaneously clearing the snow from neighbor's driveways, shopping for the infirm, and doing small car repairs at which he was adept. Even mediating squabbles between neighbors, the usual about noisy parties or a troublesome dog. The local Democratic Party machine asked him to run for councilman, an offer which he declined with a smile and expression of humility. All this was before his arrest, of course. But even after the damning publicity, neighbors rallied to his defense. Offering to testify on his behalf at his trial, as character witness for this accused killer of sixteen men.

I was twelve-years-old at the time and as shocked and confused as them.

Chapter 5

A child's life revolves around their family and friends. I still had a few friends after my father's arrest but no real family. Joe had been my family. My mother, Holly, had been largely absent.

As an adult I began thinking how ironic it was that my maternal grandmother had named her only daughter Holly. This, to indicate her conviction that her spirit would be holy, that she might even become a nun but certainly not the woman she became. Still, as the old saying goes, "The child is father of the man," so the parenting that my mother received must have been less than ideal. Her father was a small-time hustler who worked on the fringes of the mob in the numbers racket. He died young, reportedly of an accident was what I was told.

My childhood home was in the northernmost part of the Bronx, a New York City borough best known as the nineteenth-century home of Edgar Allen Poe and twentieth-century movies of the City's crime-ridden, burning borough during those years when its bankruptcy threatened. But these events hadn't affected my family with its neatly tended lawn, new car yearly, and increasing stash in my piggy bank.

Twelve years is the cusp of adolescence when I should have been concerned with thoughts of independence, choosing a vocation, and my first period. Which would have been less scary were my mother more involved with me than her lover. It came without warning except for a mild cramping, though with much fear at the sight of blood on my panty. Then it was my paternal grandmother who lessened my fear by providing instruction: how to tell when my period was coming; that it would last a few days and to keep track of them; to not worry since the blood lost was only a few tablespoons; to carry a tampon and, if lacking one when it's needed, to fold up a bunch of toilet paper to place in my underwear to soak up the blood, and to carry a sweater to wrap around my waist.

"Don't be embarrassed or feel guilty. Everyone who has a period has accidentally bled on their underwear or clothes sometime," she supportively said. And with far greater concern than I ever saw in my mother, I thought many years later.

Chapter 6

They say that fame is sought by the young but I didn't welcome mine, having become a poster child for all that was wrong with society. This, despite being an "A" student whose favored activity was reading. My paternal grandmother (bless her memory!) read to me when I was a toddler and I learned to read quickly. Advancing from Disney picture books to (as children say) chapter books and, soon after ten, onto adult fare: spy stories of danger and escape and romantic novels of loving families. The first type to thrill me, the second to maintain hope that a happier family than mine existed.

No parent would have given me the book which I found in the attic and cherished. Published in 1941, it is the autobiography of a German communist, Jan Valtin (aka Richard Krebs), and described his worldwide activities after World War I as a propagandist and thug which led to his imprisonment. First in San Quentin and later in a Nazi concentration camp from which he was freed by convincing his jailers of his change of philosophy and willingness to work for them.

After leaving prison, with his wife and baby son being held as hostage, he rejoined the Communists who soon turned against him, leading him to escape to America. Here, he wrote the best-seller, *Out Of The Night,* which, one might say, served as a blueprint for my life. Though hopefully not too closely since Valtin's wife was murdered.

My second inspiring reading, Elia Kazan's novel, *The Arrangement,* tells of a man's journey from misery to craziness to contentment. Which is all that I ever permitted myself to hope to achieve in mine.

Chapter 7

Only now, having a loving husband and impending child, did I realize that loneliness had marked my earlier life. Falsely believing myself part of a normal family I had ignored the anxious glances of neighbors as we strolled and my mother's frequent absences. I could not believe otherwise having but a child's mentality.

Only two young children lived nearby: Maria and Vincent. I was two months older than Maria and three years younger than Vincent, causing him to ignore us. Moreover, being girls we had different interests, imaginary play with dolls and fashion rather than sports. The differences in our home lives only briefly impressed me. Children aren't sociologists. day-to-day survival being their goal.

That I how use the term "survival" reveals that I must have been what is now considered an "anxious child" though, of course, not then realizing this. Trying to control my life as best I could, which may be why my preferred activity was reading in my room. A haven where I immersed myself in the lives of fearless adventurers so unlike me.

When not reading I watched old classic movies that I found in the basement: black-and-white films of struggle and love, overcoming great odds and redemption. *Casablanca* and *Gunga Din* and *The Best Years of Our Lives*. Tales of struggles for life and love. Could I have understood more than I realized?

My analyst insists on the importance of recurring dreams and one comes to mind. A simple dream in which nothing ever happens except that there is something which I can't tolerate seeing lest it destroy me. Whether hidden behind a door or down a corridor, I instantly awake before seeing it. Could it symbolize the truth about my family which I want to avoid knowing or something else? If so, why does it continue and what do I fear realizing *now*?

Chapter 8

Like all psychoanalysts, Doctor Hess doesn't pressure me. Apparently holding the attitude that what isn't realized now will be understood during later treatment. Being more patient than me but more knowledgeable since, as months passed, my nightmare *did* change. I still awoke screaming but now saw the object which terrified me. It was a guillotine, ready to chop off my head.

"What are your associations?" Doctor Hess asked after I described this dream.

"I have none," I said honestly, my mind having blanked.

He nodded and said nothing.

"That I'd be killed," I blurted, with a sudden thought.

"You've had this dream since childhood. What awful thing could a child do to warrant the death penalty, particularly with a mechanism which was never used in America and not in France for decades?"

"I don't know. Maybe the dream originated in a crime movie I shouldn't have seen."

Doctor Hess' face showed disapproval but he didn't condemn my naive statement. Psychoanalysts won't. He just repeated what he told me when I began treatment.

"Dreams are created by the unconscious, using daily events to create stories. Nightmares are motivated by trauma, like a plane crash or mugging. They tell us what most troubles us but in disguised form, like a mystery movie one must figure out. We'll learn the meaning of your dream together when you're ready. You're no longer alone,"

Hearing this I began crying. Why do I cry? I had asked myself. I never cried.

Chapter 9

"What is your earliest memory?" Doctor. Hess had asked and my mind blanked. I had no memories earlier than my father's trial and execution though knowing that I must. Everyone has *some* childhood memories no matter how few. One suddenly popped into my mind.

"I was at the house of a friend living next door. We often played and I was allowed to simply walk over. There was a large white shed in the backyard and I walked toward it to look in its window."

"Don't go inside. There's a lion there," a workman who had been mowing the lawn called out.

I frantically ran home, only years later realizing that I'd been the subject of a cruel joke.

"What associations does a lion bring to your mind?" Doctor Hess asked.

"A ferocious creature with huge teeth to devour," I said quickly.

"And?"

"Maybe it was the feeling I had from living in my family."

Dating hasn't been easy for me despite my conventional good looks: tall, thin, and blond though with small breasts. One can't have everything I'd often reassured myself.

My first boyfriend, long before physical characteristics were considered important, arrived at age five. Even in kindergarten girls had boasted. "He kissed me on the lips," a lisping classmate smilingly told me.

Because of my birthday I was the smallest in my class and often teased. "You're small," girls would say when not criticizing my hair or clothes. Once, upon returning home crying, my mother advised me. "The next time someone calls you 'small' say, 'You're just mad because your mom's a ho.'"

"What?" I asked, not understanding, and my grandmother cried, "No, no, no!"

My mother had looked smug and my father smiled. That was the kind of family it was.

Chapter 10

A person living in a burning house has no time to ponder the circumstances. Survival must be their only possible goal and I survived, gaining the best grades in my classes and being what is derogatively termed "teacher's pet." I had no bosom friends but how could I? Neighbors feared my father, their wives feared my mother, and I couldn't communicate. Not from a speech defect but because I'd never learned to share feelings, having survived by chopping off mine. Which isn't a good way to live and I vowed that if I ever had children they would do better.

I now live with my husband, Brian, in a house that we were lucky to have before COVID and crime pushed Manhattanites into home offices and the suburbs. Among these, Scardale was a top choice for several reasons. Having barely eighteen-thousand residents, it has a sparse suburban sense, many restaurants and coffee shops, and an exceptionally low crime rate.

As you might expect it's an expensive place to live, its average annual family income being a little over five-hundred-thousand-dollars. We can afford it because of an inheritance from my father who had the good sense to place forty-million-dollars into a trust that I could access at twenty-one. He also provided for my mother though not in the style she wanted. It had taken her possible last lover, who became her next husband, to do that.

Brian grew up in Scarsdale and we live in the house that he inherited. Also a lawyer, he has the dubious honor of being the only grandson of the deceased managing partner of the firm which gained me court approval to witness my father's execution, which is an exceptional party talking point that we've never used.

Chapter 11

My father's execution made me a media sensation. Not as greatly as happens today but enough to keep me isolated. My grandmother's solution was to have me home-schooled, which turned out well. I was always an avid reader and she hired tutors for the subjects that I had difficulty learning on my own such as math. So I learned calculus, a college subject, before graduating high school.

My Scholastic Aptitude Test (SAT) scores got me into Barnard College: a math score of seven-ninety and an EBRW (Evidence Based Reading and Writing) score of seven-sixty. The total score of fifteen-hundred-sixty placed me in the ninety-ninth percentile of test-takers. My dad would have been proud.

Barnard was a good choice. Being in Manhattan and across the street from Columbia University enabled me to live at home and travel to classes, avoiding intrusive questions and hurtful comments from dormitory-living students.

By adopting disguises of pious Muslim and disheveled homeless, I avoided the few paparazzi for whom my photo was still considered potential income, carrying conventional student dress in an oversized bag and changing in a school bathroom. None questioned my appearance, unconventionally dressed people being part of Manhattan's landscape.

I got good grades at Barnard too, graduating with a three-point-nine average. Apart from the required Physical Education requirement which I declined by being a cheerleader, my collegiate years were painless, like high school but requiring a subway ride. Law School was different.

Chapter 12

My experience at Columbia Law School was probably like what I would have experienced at any law school with one exception. The first required class, Legal Methods, took place the beginning of law school proper and lasted three weeks. It was liked by all, being taken on a no-sweat pass/fail basis. Afterward, when grades became important, students fretted over not getting an "A" and there was a daily grind of morning and afternoon classes followed by readings required for the next day. Later came the need to create outlines of courses as study aids for the open-book exams.

My inheritance enabled me to avoid the other demands on student time: seeking a summer job and speaking with a career counselor. The first because of my financial independence, the second because I had no sense what I wanted to do after graduation, lacking the usual desire to work for a law firm or as a public defender. A person having little contact with their feelings tends to drift, seeking a favorable wind. Other students cared about their transcript; I cared about my disguise, which turned out to be less than perfect.

To avoid fellow-students who adopted a kinship feeling and the student social activists who seemed to popular every Broadway corner, I avoided on-campus lounges, hanging out at the Ortomare Ristorante Pizzeria which is arguably the best restaurant in the neighborhood. That it was Italian helped make it my home away from home.

I spent many evenings eating and studying there, simultaneously hungering for human contact but fearing intimacy. Doctor Hess called this *compartmentalization*: creating social barriers to keep me from being hurt. Which makes sense but didn't work for long.

Chapter 13

The stranger was the epitome of correctness as he stood beside my table and asked, "May I sit here?"

Looking up warily from my text, I inspected him closely. Trust was absent in my character but the restaurant was packed. To refuse his courteous request could have made my presence less welcome by the proprietor and my loss.

My casual agreement changed my life in ways that I couldn't have imagined though, given my heritage, this might have reflected ignorance of my underlying nature.

While continuing my study I heard him order Salmone al Salmoriglio (salmon with spinach and roasted potatoes). I had ordered this too.

Though seeming to ignore me while eating, he noted my text.

"Are you a lawyer?" he asked amiably.

It would have been rude not to respond and, as I said, occupying a lone table in a usually packed restaurant for hours wasn't a favor that I wanted to lose.

"No. I'm a student at Columbia Law," I said.

"I studied at its Business School thirty years ago. We were all nerds then. The atmosphere is probably different now."

My reason for speaking with him was simple: I was lonely and tired of studying. My only honest social contact was with my loving grandmother. I had no other companion in the world.

"It must be! There's a social activist on every corner sporting everything from a billboard to a mattress. It's why this restaurant is my nightly haunt. The owner doesn't object, maybe because we're both Italian."

"I'm Italian but wouldn't have thought you were," he said.

"My Nordic features came from my mother, a Swedish model and whore," I blurted and instantly shut up, feeling overwhelming embarrassment.

Dead To Life

Though what I said was true, it was far from what one shares, and particularly with a stranger.

Chapter 14

The stranger didn't say anything for a few moments and when he did it was with a pained expression.

"I'm sorry. Children deserve good parents though not all get them. One hears terrible stories of torture and murder by parents," he said.

I didn't reply, not knowing what to say and still feeling embarrassed. He seemed to sense this and remained silent. Behaving like Doctor Hess did years later. Then he made a revealing statement though whether intentional or deliberate I haven't decided even now.

"I didn't have good parents either. My father died young. A heart attack was the medical examiner's judgment but I always doubted it. They had a violent marriage and I think she poisoned him, leaving me with an unhealed wound."

Our meals were forgotten. The raised voices of customers cocooned us, feeling lost in our pasts. I reached out my hand but, sensibly, he didn't respond. For a strange man to place his hand on a woman's would push her away and not closer. The gap in age would have made intimacy impossible and he wouldn't want me to believe it was what he sought. Years later, when considering that moment, I wondered about the distinction between sensitivity and cleverness. Did he really care? Was his story even true?

I later learned that his story *was* true though I never could decide if he cared. But at that moment I wanted to believe this and did. Our togetherness went undisturbed by the waiter who stood respectfully at our table.

"Would you like anything before we close?" he asked with a hint of discomfort.

The man turned toward me, making me feel as if I were his daughter and I shook my head.

"Put both on my account," he said, and the waiter scurried away.

"No," I said softly, looking into his eyes.

"Please. I haven't spoken so in years and needed it. Will you be here tomorrow night?"

"Yes. School ends in two months. I study here most nights."

"Until then," he said with a smile, and handed me a business card from his wallet. His name was Leonardo and he was a "Financial Consultant." Which can mean anything, I thought. Instead of academic credential the only other text on the card read, "6P Rule: Proper Planning Prevents Piss-Poor Performance." I was impressed. It would have been rude not to respond in a friendly fashion.

"I'm Annika," I said, reaching out a hand.

We shook and he mused aloud, "I have a grand-daughter named Annika. It's of Hausa and Hebrew origin, meaning 'sweet-faced' and favored by God.'"

I sat staring after he left.

Chapter 15

"Why did you choose to become a lawyer?" Doctor Hess asked during one of our early sessions.

My mind blanked at his understandable question though it is one that is often asked.

Why did I decide to be a lawyer? Maybe because of the stories that Abraham told me. He was my father's friend and lawyer for many years, doing the paperwork for such civil matters as buying a house and taxes.

Abraham was my father's age though with gray hair that made him look older. He was long divorced and childless and often told me stories during his visits. Some were his of childhood experiences but many were of the legal life, humorous tales of dumb lawyering behavior. These convinced me that even I, with my toilet level self-esteem, could be a lawyer. Some of his stories were of lawyers who finally discovered their true calling later in life.

After fortifying my with the favored snack he always brought, dark chocolate enrobed-raspberry filled cookies, he dramatically told of a lawyer who hated law and loved music. "Many lawyers dream of escape but few do," Abraham said as an introduction. "This lawyer barely scraped by after leaving his legal job, rooming with and fed by friends working at law firms. He found that making it on Broadway was far riskier than making partner at a law firm but persisted, earning pocket money by writing commercial jingles. That was before his comic treatment of life in 1970s Texas was made into a hit movie."

"Did he regret going to law school?" I had asked Abraham.

"No. He said the three years there gave him time to grow up."

"Was it the same for you, that law school gave you the time to grow up?" Doctor Hess had asked me.

Dead To Life

"Probably," I said, after a long silence.

Chapter 16

Yet how much socially *had* I grown up while attending Law School I wondered? Not much since my fellow students had remained barely acknowledged acquaintances rather than friends and I was cold with the boys who expressed interest. My only continuing companion had been Leonardo who was thirty-years older and which may have been why I tolerated our relationship. Also because his statements were uncritical and accepting, like those of my loving grandmother.

Leonardo educated me about life, smoothing my ragged edges. "You shouldn't have slapped him," he gently advised when I confessed an incident. A fellow student that wanted to date me had grabbed my hand as I left him. "If I had a gun I might have shot him," I angrily told Leonardo.

"Which would destroy your brilliant future. Always consider the consequences before acting. Behaving impulsively isn't a virtue," he said.

"Did you take his advice?" Doctor Hess asked.

"I always took Leonardo's advice," I said.

"Why?"

"Because he became like a father to me, and he loved me."

"He loved you?" Doctor Hess asked evenly.

"Well, he never condemned me and he always gave good advice and never tried getting money from me. In fact he always paid for our meals and bought me an expensive presents: a leather Saint Laurent shoulder bag and silver cable bracelet. That was to celebrate my article being accepted by the Columbia Law Review. It opposed legally designating extremist groups as domestic terrorist organizations."

"Costly gifts for a casual acquaintance," Doctor Hess mused.

"Not really. Considering the size of my inheritance their price was less than doughnut money," I sniffed.

Chapter 17

A student's life is never fully occupied no matter how much homework they get. They must eat and sleep and remain cordial to other barely sane students while pondering the profession's failures. One example had been the decision of a Family Court judge who returned a child to their abusing mother despite opposition from the Child Protective Services agency and mental health professionals. After the girl was murdered by her mother, my teacher said that the judge possessed superb legal credentials but lacked common sense.

When I shared this story with Leonardo he remarked, "Common sense isn't common nor always sensible. You doubt this?" he asked when I looked puzzled.

"I'm not smart enough to doubt anything you say. Just wondering why I hadn't behaved sensibly in my life," I replied.

"In what part? I know little about you except for what was reported after you became a media sensation."

I said nothing for a long moment, feeling blocked and unable to speak. Then I told him my biggest secret, something that shamed me all my life. Convincing me that I was crazy and making me avoid people, believing that none would understand.

Yet then, in a bustling restaurant, I shared my secret with the first person, a recent stranger, who I felt would understand. Maybe it takes one whose mother poisoned their father, I thought and giggled.

"What's funny?" Leonardo asked softly.

"Why I'm going to tell you since you're likely the only person who would understand," I said.

Chapter 18

"Why would Leonardo be the only person who could understand?" Doctor Hess had asked.

"Because he had such a childhood too. His mother poisoned his father," I said.

My confession to Leonardo, which was how it felt, didn't take long. It concerned not murder or even of theft but of nightmares.

"My mother left my father when I was seven. Years later I was told that she returned to Sweden with a wealthy boyfriend. I never heard from her again and never tried finding her.

"My most vivid memory of her is a recurring nightmare I've had since childhood. I'm lying in bed and she's atop me, holding my wrists with one hand and rubbing my vulvae with her other. When I wake screaming there are marks on my wrists where in the dream she held me down. I learned in biology that the mind can move blood to parts of the body."

"You often have this dream?" Leonardo asked gently.

"Yes, and another which comes less often, sometimes not for weeks. In it a guillotine lies behind a door or around a corridor. It's something that I can't bear seeing since if I do I'll be destroyed, explode or something. But nothing ever happens. I never see it and no one ever dies in the dream. It seems there's something terrifying which I can't tolerate seeing it. When I wake up I cover my head with a blanket and fear getting out of bed.

"Now, if there's the story of an execution in a newspaper or magazine, I must quickly throw it out. Yet I also feel compelled to read it and I *chose* capital punishment appeals for my class assignment. I've always felt weird. Could *any* boyfriend tolerate a woman who wakes up screaming and feels compelled to read about her greatest fear?"

I looked down during the silence that followed, afraid that confessing had ended my only real friendship.

Chapter 19

But Leonardo didn't recoil from me as I feared. Instead, he seemed to understand my suffering and why I had long been alone.

"You suffered. But am a survivor like me," he said softly.

The restaurant emptied as we lingered over coffee. Espresso for him and regular for me. "Alcohol is an acquired taste that's best left un-acquired," he had said during our first meeting.

Years later Doctor Hess explained that dreams are symbolic and interpreted by associating to their content. Leonardo knew this despite lacking the benefit of psychotherapy. "I read a lot," he said.

"You have two recurring nightmares. That both are filled with emotion indicate you're trying to tell yourself something important, Would you object if I told you *my* association?" Leonardo asked after moments of silence,

"Anything to have them stop!" I burst out.

"What do you remember from your earlier years, before the age of five or so?"

"Virtually nothing," I replied.

Again Leonardo paused, as if fearing the effect of what he would say. I sipped coffee and waited.

"I think your mother molested you and you wanted to kill her. That your unconscious created the execution dream to remind you of the punishment for murder and keep you from doing it."

Chapter 20

I initially said nothing after hearing Leonardo's theory. Nor did my face betray emotion despite feeling like I'd been punched in the gut since I instinctively knew that what he said was true: my mother *had* molested me and I *had* wanted to kill her.

"You're right," I said finally, looking away and fearing to face him.

"Holding such secrets would make anyone feel weird," he said supportively.

"You should know," I said angrily, before apologizing.

"I'm sorry. "You're trying to help me. What happened to me isn't your fault."

"That's all right, I'm used to it. Being innocent isn't exactly my nature."

"So now that I know their meaning will the nightmares go away?" I asked.

Though not being a doctor, he was my expert on dreaming at that moment.

"Maybe, from what I've read. Since you sense the interpretation to be accurate they should stop, or be less frequent and intense."

Before leaving the restaurant that evening I hugged him for the first time. Feeling gratitude but also needing to understand our relationship.

Aways distrustful, I wondered who Leonardo was, this stranger with whom I shared secrets. Was he who he'd stated and the story of his life true? Or was it pretense, designed to entice me into some scheme for his benefit? Was our friendship real or intended to foster my dependence on him before he betrayed me.

Betrayal fascinated me, having sensed that I'd been the object of betrayal all my life. But *how*, I asked myself, since I had never doubted that my father loved me *and only me* except from his mother.

Lawyers learn to view matters from different angles, and to always assume that their client isn't completely truthful. Has Leonardo been honest or am I the dupe and he the string puller? I asked myself, suddenly feeling that I had been living in an imaginative bubble.

Yet one belief felt certain: that I could understand Leonardo only by investigating him, as does every lawyer with every opponent.

Chapter 21

Weeks before, I learned in my Legal Methods class the obligations of a criminal defense lawyer to their client. To never rely only on statements from law enforcement about what happened since police officers can lie and prosecutors do exaggerate. That even when evidence seems overwhelming, the independent interviews of witnesses and other investigations may find unexpected material to impeach the state's witnesses.

That a criminal lawyer's job is not just to protect their client's constitutional rights or mediate between client and government to obtain the best plea agreement, but to win their case using all legal and ethical means available with winning meaning a dismissal of charges, an acquittal at trial, or an outcome that the client can accept.

But my goal was simpler: to discover who Leonardo *really* is, whether a genial, lonely man or more.

I've long thought that my greatest strength is awareness of my limitations, being free to admit and remedy them. So, knowing nothing about swindlers, I did research and learned how gullible people can be when un-earned riches are promised.

Thirty-years ago one swindler created a company which allegedly made computer memory cards. After its stock quickly rose four-hundred-fifty-one-percent, customers were defrauded of forty-million-dollars. Using phony invoices instead of memory cards, his customers were sent fruit baskets. Now *that* took nerve!

Another crook ran a hugely successful penny-stock scam, buying large amounts of worthless stock to drive up their price before selling his shares. After pleading guilty to fraud he was jailed for twenty-two months of a four-year jail sentence. His later exploits were more notable than most such compatriots:

writing a memoir that was made into a hit movie and becoming a sought-after motivational speaker.

My interest waned after reading about them. Though gypsters are necessarily warm and engaging, few likely possessed the psychological knowledge exhibited by Leonardo. Or could it be that I don't want to think badly of him, I wondered.

Chapter 22

"What do you know about Greta Garbo?" Doctor Hess had asked.

"Only that she was a famous movie star of the nineteen-thirties," I said.

I was puzzled by his question though knowing from his wall posters that he was a movie buff.

"Before becoming a star she was the quiet, gawky Swedish Greta Gustafson. Hollywood reduced that complex creature into the sullen Greta Garbo who became every man's fantasy mistress, worshipped by the entire world. Being secure in her position not because she was beautiful, which is a matter of taste, but because she became a superhuman symbol of The Other Woman. Maybe something like that happened to you. You were young when your father was executed and, hungering for another, projected your desire onto this older, friendly man who became the father you needed. Which role, being skilled and clever, he adopted."

"I loved Leonardo, "I said softly.

"You did, and I think he loved you too."

"But I betrayed him," I murmured.

"Because he betrayed you too," Doctor Hess said. "Leonardo was something dropped from heaven, a visitation to grace your life, maybe even to protect you from the depression that might have caused suicide. I won't deprecate this by pointing out its conventionality to many movies. A young girl loves her father and he loves her, until he's gone and she spends the following years striding through rooms looking beautiful and glacial."

"I wanted more than that," I said.

"You did, and that's why you investigated Leonardo."

"But not seriously at first. I didn't want to know."

"Oliver Wendell Holmes, one of the greatest American jurists, wrote, 'Where we love is home, home that our feet may leave but not our hearts."

I remained silent as he continued.

"He also wrote, 'It's faith in something and enthusiasm for something that makes life worth living. The great thing in this world is not so much where we are but in which direction we are moving.' You were moving on from your father and Leonardo."

"Yes, I think I was," I agreed.

Chapter 23

Possessing no background in investigation, Leonardo's reflected not Sherlock Holmes but my erroneous image of private eyes. In my mind, thanks to the many books and movies I'd consumed, they worked in dimly lit offices, awaiting clients who were usually endangered or had a problem outside the jurisdiction of police. Their job was to gain evidence of wrong-doing and right wrongs, hopefully without getting shot. For this they used disguises, lies, surveillance tools and searches, unbothered by the niceties of legality. When caught, they wriggled out of trouble and solved the case to their client's undying gratitude.

Now, with the benefits of greater sanity, I realize how foolish I'd been. Why hadn't I hired a licensed private investigator instead of playing Nancy Drew? Because then I was emotionally still a teenager, a creature who believed they know everything.

I began my investigation with Leonardo's card which contained the name and address of his company and a hustling business quotation. Then, late one night when he was unlikely to be around, I went to the address on the card. Which, to my surprise, wasn't an office building but a townhouse on Manhattan's Upper East Side.

After strolling by it I retreated to an all-night diner and checked its past sales notice on a real estate app. The information impressed me!

His limestone townhouse had been built in 1908 and recently renovated, it contained six bedrooms, nine baths, a steam sauna, three wood-burning fireplaces, a terrace, and a laundry room. Its price would have taken most of my forty-million-dollar inheritance. Where did Leonardo get his money? I wondered.

Chapter 24

My research was short-circuited by Leonardo. As we left the restaurant one evening, he invited me to lunch at his home.

"It's quieter and I boast that my cook is the best in the City," he said.

Noting my hesitation he added, "You and your grandmother, of course."

I didn't reply as we waved goodbye but he was used to my idiosyncrasies. A good friendship is when one tolerates the other's shortcomings, as he did. Still, I had hesitated despite sensing that he lacked romantic interest in me. Like I said, my self-esteem was in the toilet.

Leah, my grandmother, had isolated herself since the death of her son so I expected her to reject Leonardo's invitation but was surprised.

"It would be good for us to get out. Roman can accompany us," she said protectively.

Roman had been my father's bodyguard and was now ours. Being orphaned at a young age and never marrying, he idolized my father. After the arrest, Roman moved into our house, helping with errands and providing a protective element on our isolated cul-de-sac in the economically deteriorating Bronx. After my father's execution and my becoming an heiress, I was glad that he was here.

I'd wanted to move to a safer part of the City or a suburb but my grandmother wouldn't hear of it. "This is our home," she insisted. Some attitudes can't be changed, I decided, and dropped the topic.

Though usually dressing casually, that evening my grandmother went nineteen-fifties formal style complete with hat. Which I welcomed since it indicated that her spirits were lifting. Children shouldn't die before their parents and my father's death hadn't wrecked only me.

The drive took a half-hour and Leonardo met us at the door. "Welcome to my home," he said. Weirdly, I instantly remembered that statement was what Count Dracula said to his unfortunate guest in the famed movie.

Chapter 25

Lunch was scheduled for 1:00 PM and we arrived twenty-minutes early. Leonardo greeted us warmly as he led us to the library.

"My home away from home," he said, gesturing toward the shelved books. Some were reachable only using a ladder hooked to the wall, a sight that I had seen only in old movies.

"May I?" I asked, nodding toward them.

"Of course. Treat this as your home," he said.

Though knowing that I shouldn't I found myself falling under his spell. It's just that you're missing your father, I told myself with a shiver.

Decorators buy books by the yard but, judging by their variety, these seemed to have been read. There were old suspense novels of Agatha Christie and modern ones by Alex Michaelides and Gillian Flynn. Old spy novels by Eric Ambler and John LeCarre and the newer horror creations of Stephen King. What surprised me were the many children's Halloween books: "How To Catch A Monster," "Don't Push The Button," "A Halloween Scare At My House" and more. Did Leonardo have children or grandchildren? I wondered. This was another mystery to solve.

To avoid being rude, I casually rejoined the others. Under Roman's scrutiny, Leonardo charmed my grandmother who was more voluble than I had seen her in a long time.

"I still miss my mother. Losing a child must be worse," Leonardo said.

"My son was such a good man. All the neighbors loved him. He kept our neighborhood safe!" she said in a cracking voice. Her eyes brimmed with tears and Leonardo took her hand.

"I understand," he said, and I knew instantly that he did.

"Did you feel he was grooming you?" Doctor Hess had asked.

"No, never. One can't live being so suspicious, believing that every statement could be a lie," I said.

"Yet there were many lies in your family. You read the transcript of your father's trial."

"But that was business, not personal. Not about *me*."

"*Business*," Doctor Hess said, and the word hung in the air.

Chapter 26

I can only think of him as "daddy" no matter what the newspapers said. For me he'll always be that. Was he also the "notorious contract killer" they wrote. Yes, though I never could believe it. How can one think that of a beloved parent, the one who soothed my hurts and listened to my nightmares, rushed me to the doctor with the smallest symptom, and read me nursery stories. He couldn't be *that* man! I told myself.

"You believed him innocent," Doctor Hess had said.

"I didn't think about it, he was so good to me. It was as if he were two people: the newspaper image and my daddy."

"Did he ever speak of his childhood?" Doctor Hess had asked.

"Rarely. Of being poor, tenement life, fights in the street until others began to fear him."

Leonardo's lunch was exceptional, fully as good as I enjoyed at Roberto's, the famed Italian restaurant in the Bronx which is less expensive than its Manhattan counterparts. Others enjoyed the Cotechino con Fagioli e Broccoli di Rapa (pork sausage, cannellini beans, and broccoli). Leonardo, respectful of my semi-vegetarian diet, had the cook prepare Mozzarella alla Caprese (mozzarella with roasted peppers, black olives, marinated mushrooms, over sliced tomato) for me.

Lunch was followed by coffee in the library during which Leonardo spoke of his early life. Growing up an only child, absent a father and close relatives. Gaining scholarships to Stanford University and the Wharton Business School of the University of Pennsylvania. Work at hedge funds followed until he went out on his own.

My grandmother and I warmed to him but Roman's face remained impassive.

"What is it?" I asked him after we arrived home.

"His stories were too smooth, too agreeable," he said.

"You don't like him, do you?" I asked.

"My job isn't liking your friends but protecting your family," he said firmly.

Chapter 27

One of my law professors once made what seemed a profound statement: "evidence isn't truth," he said, and of Leonardo I had neither. Checking his academic credentials, work history, and more were elementary tasks and he did own the mansion that we visited. But this didn't mean he was honest in other ways since I had no way to check the personal details. Had his mother really murdered his father? Was he a battler as a child? Moreover, did these mean any more than he had suffered like so many children. Though not me since I had my father's love until he was gone.

My next idea derived from an episode of the long running TV series, *Blue Bloods,* which I avidly watched. Reveling in its image of a happy extended family led by the Chief of the New York City Police Department. Though they were Irish and we were Italian, the similarity of family dynamics was close, apart from their weekly crises of course.

The show is a modern Western set in New York City in which goodness wins over evil. In one episode, a young woman detective adopts the disguise of a prostitute to capture the serial killer targeting them. Why not, wearing a disguise, chat up Leonardo's past fellow students and co-workers to gain information about him? I thought. And the more I did, the better I liked this idea until remembering the episode's ending: that even though the detective had protective colleagues who I lacked, she was nearly killed. I needed protection and knew that Roman would provide it.

Chapter 28

I opened an account at *LinkedIn*, the website for hustling workers. Using an alias despite a software guru's insistence that privacy is now an illusion. There, I settled on twenty names from Leonardo's graduate school class and hedge fund. Though he had no listing, these mentioned his name. For an obvious reason I chose men in their twenties and thirties. While their marital status wasn't stated, they would more likely be single and attracted by the slut uniform I'd viewed on a *Blue Bloods* episode.

My profile was of a college senior majoring in economics who sought information about the working conditions at hedge funds and consulting firms. My posted photo, braless and tightly sweatered, bordered on pornography and my wait was brief.

Thomas, my first responder, was a twenty-nine-year-old hedge fund analyst living in Beekman Place. A ritzy, well-policed area just north of the United Nations complex, I had unsuccessfully tried to persuade my grandmother to move there.

His response was sweet: "I empathize with your confusion. It seems only yesterday that I worried whether my huge student loan could be paid, and likely never if staying underemployed and lacking a well-paid spouse.

"I worked at Leonardo's company before jumping to a bigger firm. E-mail isn't for serious communication. We're both in the City so why not meet for coffee?"

Why not, I thought.

Chapter 29

Not being totally stupid, I told Roman my plan.

"You distrust Leonardo and so do I. I've dug online and found men that knew him. To get information I plan to meet each and would like you to watch from a distance. They seem fine but one can never be sure."

"I don't like it," he said.

"I didn't think you would but it's what I must do."

"When you're so determined you sound like your father."

Trying to keep from tearing up at his mention of my father I said, "I am determined and I need your help."

"Of course," he said.

Which *wasn't* a simple "of course" since his required lessons followed. "Unexpected situations arise without notice so you must know how to defend yourself," he said.

The techniques I learned aren't nice but are effective. To use my fingers or any sharp object to hurt the eye which causes unbearable pain and assures escape. To keep my fingers straight and close together, with thumb tucked and bent at the knuckle, before striking under the attacker's nose or into their neck where carotid artery and jugular vein lay. That striking a man's groin causes instant pain, loss of breath, and falling to the ground. That kicking the side of his knee causes loss of balance. During my last lesson he emphasized the need to leverage my body weight, and the defensive value of everyday objects like keys, pens, and hairspray.

Finally, he asked, "How do you feel now?"

"Confident!" I said firmly, and he smiled.

Chapter 30

Believing it important to assert control from the start, I invited Thomas to meet that Friday at 5:30PM at Little Collins, a mid-town coffee house close by his job. The shop's outdoor seating would give Roman the ability to watch us unobtrusively and its 8:00PM closing was later than many such establishments.

Thomas agreed and arrived first as we watched from the car. "I can take him easily," Roman said glumly.

He still didn't like my plan.

"OK, but let me speak with him first," I joked.

Roman didn't smile. My dad hadn't kept him around for his sense of humor.

Thomas was tall, blond, and clean-shaven. His clothes weren't that of the company big-shots who lectured occasionally at my law school: suit, white shirt, suitable tie, and black shoes. Dress, I had learned, was more casual at venture-capital and private equity firms where simple slacks and button-up shirt are the norm.

My slutty dress, a black one-piece cowl mini-dress was clearly a hit for his welcoming smile lingered on my breasts. We sedately shook hands and entered the shop. After giving our orders, Thomas said he would grab a space in the outside seating area, there being only small space between the indoor tables.

I joined him ten-minutes later carrying a tray with my blueberry scone and green tea and his coffee and turkey confit sandwich, he having said that he'd skipped lunch. Those seated around us seemed a mix of tourists and locals. *Roman will be pleased there are no heavies* was my silly thought.

As we spoke Thomas' focus went from my breasts to my face. Thankfully, he didn't mention my striking dress. *That*, this alleged college senior wouldn't know how to explain.

Chapter 31

"Have you decided where you want to work?" Thomas asked.

My story was of being just another clueless college student who will hold one of the hundred-thousand economic degrees awarded that year. That I'd read of venture capital and consulting firms being the biggest hirers so I was checking them out before throwing my hat in the ring.

"But not only the hat," Thomas said with a smile.

We both knew what was on his mind though sleeping with him wouldn't happen. Not from any moral principle since he could be a potential mate but because it would then take more time to return his thinking to my goal. Also, Roman was watching and I didn't know how far his concept of "protection" went. Thomas didn't deserve a beating.

"I'm not sure," I said, ignoring the implication. "I heard Leonardo's company could be a good start and maybe more. What do you think?"

The company was so well known that its business name wasn't needed. Thomas' reaction wasn't what I expected.

"I worked there for a year. He's brilliant," he said, after a pause.

Though appearing reticent to speak, I sensed more was coming and waited.

"I'll tell you a story," he said finally. "Hedge funds are big on athletics and field teams to compete. I'd boxed in college so was automatically placed on theirs, winning two matches before losing the third to a friend at another firm. Right after the fight Leonardo asked if I knew why I'd lost. I said I didn't and he said it was because I lacked the killing instinct, that I hadn't *hated* my opponent. He fired me a week later, saying I wasn't aggressive enough and he wanted killers. Are *you* a killer?"

Am I? I wondered.

Chapter 32

Thomas didn't give me time to answer.

"Now I remember why you seemed familiar. *You're that girl*, the one who watched her father's execution. You poor kid," he said.

Feeling surprised at being recognized I blurted, "It was long ago, a rough time."

"I'll bet. Why did you want to go? I'm sorry. That's an indelicate question."

"But understandable and exactly what reporters asked," I said.

I considered what to say during the long pause that followed, having always avoided pondering this question. The answer that came was more ordinary than many would expect. Certainly not curiosity or whatever.

"He loved me and I loved him," I said.

"I can understand. My parents were God-awful but I could never escape the delusion they loved me. And maybe they did, in their way and as best they could."

"How were they awful?" I asked, wanting to regain control of the conversation.

"By not parenting. Real parents teach their kids how to brush their teeth and comb their hair. Don't get me wrong: they fed and clothed me and called a doctor when needed. My father left the parenting to my mother and did what she said. She was pretty and narcissistic and he was a loner without friends. But he worked hard and supported us. He'd been a boxer as a teenager and taught me to love the sport. Warmth and closeness were absent. I was never hugged as a child except when being sick which thankfully was rare."

"I'm sorry," I said, feeling overwhelmed by his deluge of words.

"At least you were loved as a child. I never was."

Chapter 33

"I *was* loved by my father but my childhood wasn't perfect," I said. "Your parents ignored you like my mother ignored me when she wasn't putting me down. 'Alison is such a beautiful child,' I heard her tell my father."

"But you're beautiful!"

"Not to her."

We basked in shared togetherness until I reminded myself why I was there.

"So what do you think about my working for Leonardo?" I asked.

"Maybe. He pays more and women better than at other companies, and has been in business for years. The benefits are great too: leased car and all-inclusive medical coverage though that's a standard Wall Street benefit. He paid off my student loan and my Manhattan hotel bill until I rented an apartment. All before he fired me, of course."

"You'll get another job," I said supportively.

"That's for sure. I have three interviews scheduled so far. Despite his peculiarities, I learned a lot from him. He has a good reputation and his company looks good on my resume. I wouldn't cross him off because of what he said and...."

"Because my father was a killer too," I said, expressing what he hesitated to say.

Thomas blushed, which was when I decided to take him to bed. How to do it with Roman being so close? I wondered, and quickly decided to be decisive like my father. But leaving the table to speak with Roman would require explanation. "The truth, or what is most believable, is always best," my father once said.

"That big man watching us is my bodyguard and part of my family since childhood. I'll tell him you're Okay," I said.

Chapter 34

Roman remained seated when I approached and sat opposite him.

"Thomas is a good guy so you needn't worry. We're going out to eat and I'll take a taxi home," I said.

"That's not how protection works. Taking a cab to the Bronx at night isn't safe," he replied, impassively.

I decided I hadn't been honest enough.

"I'll be spending the night at his apartment. You've trained me and I have the Pain Pen too," I said.

The Pain Pen gives discreet protection, being a small, pink twenty-five-million-volt stun gun resembling a pen. I don't know if it was this or my tone of voice that did it but Roman didn't argue. He simply got up and walked toward the exit, giving Thomas a steely look as he passed.

"I wouldn't want to be on his wrong side," Thomas said as I sat beside him and his eyes returned to my breasts.

"Why don't we go somewhere to eat," I suggested. Another woman might have said, "Let's go to you apartment and fuck," but that wasn't me.

"What restaurant do you have in mind?"

"I come from a frugal family. We can get deli and eat in your apartment," I said.

I got no argument, only his surprised look as we left the coffee shop to find a taxi.

Chapter 35

Our taxi waited outside the deli as we ordered: a chicken salad sandwich for me and The Terminator Sandwich (turkey, lettuce, tomato, mustard) for him. Its name made me nervous as I thought of Roman's suspicions. "Silly, isn't it?" Thomas said, and I just smiled.

His apartment was on East Fiftieth Street, just north of the United Nations complex. The building was built as the 1929 Depression began and hurriedly rented. "The walls aren't the greatest since construction was rushed but apart from that I love it. It's quiet with nice neighbors though all work hard and we hardly see one another. I met everyone during the recent fire," Thomas said.

"Huh?" I exclaimed.

"Not as bad as it sounds," he said, with a smile. "A tenant cooking on his balcony sent smoke pouring through the building and everyone ran downstairs congregating outside. My neighbor had banged on doors yelling 'fire.' If not for the cry he would have been ignored. One doesn't open the door to strangers in the City."

"No," I agreed.

The apartment's two entrances, one through the kitchen into the living room and the other entered it through a small foyer, gave it an old-fashioned charm though the furnishings were typical Ikea. A media console held a huge TV and bookcases. Opposite was a sectional sofa with reversible chaise lounge and two swivel accent chairs. The bedroom held little more than a bed.

"I'm not much into decorating," Thomas said.

"That's OK. Neither am I," I said.

Being a virgin, my knowledge of romance came from the novels I read with all stressing that men don't like critical women.

After showing me around we adjourned to the kitchen. Though the food was commendable, conversation took center stage.

I chose tea over the wine he offered, being leery of addling my brain more than it was. This was good since Thomas' question was unexpected.

"What would your bodyguard do if I was fresh?" he asked with a grin.

"His name is Roman. What do you think?" I blurted.

Chapter 36

We ate quickly before getting down to business, his and mine. His being getting into my panties and mine being to penetrate his mind. What he'd told me about Leonardo was informative but I felt sure he knew more. What he considered gossip could be significant but asking wouldn't work. Pillow talk might, if the spy novels I'd read were accurate.

When we finished eating, as I obediently washed dishes in a wifely manner, he cradled his arms around me and kissed the back of my neck. I turned off the faucet and leaned back into his chest. What happened next was predictable except for his hesitation. In the novels it was the man who was aggressive but this role seemed to fall to me.

Peeling off my dress took moments and my bra and panties just a little longer. But then, as I stood naked, he simply stared without moving, remaining fully clothed. Only when I began removing his tie did he begin undressing.

Roman's Pain Pen wouldn't provide the protection I then needed. Being the prepared, cautious soul that father trained me to be, I had earlier bought LifeStyles SKYN condoms from Amazon, an online review having describing them as being "softer and more skinlike," in the "generous-fit" option considering Thomas' height.

Once in bed, I handed him a packet of condoms and said, "Put this on. I'm not getting pregnant."

He did, and activity progressed.

Chapter 37

All happened quickly though I didn't know this until later, it being my first time.

After penetration he burst out, "You feel great!"

I'd been told by my gynecologist that I was "small" but didn't grasp its value until then.

Thomas jerked twice before shuddering and rolling off me.

"How was it for you?" he asked gently. This question strengthened my feeling that inviting myself to his apartment wasn't a mistake.

"Wonderful!" I exclaimed, though my only feeling had been of my body being invaded. I knew from novels that enjoying sex can take time and depend on the relationship with the partner. Happening quicker in a loving relationship and never when sex is considered a duty.

But that evening my goal hadn't been pleasure but the useful information that Thomas might reveal during pillow talk. I hadn't expected what he said next.

"Move in with me."

His request left me feeling adrift, like a sailor whose boat suddenly begins sinking. This wasn't in any book I'd read.

Because lengthy silence would indicate rejection and end my investigation, I said the first thing that came to mind, ignoring its clash of image with my slutwear.

"I can't leave my grandma now. I and Roman are all she has," I said sorrowfully.

But this was enough and maybe forgotten by Thomas as he began Round Two. Which *was* enjoyable unlike Round One.

Chapter 38

While Thomas dozed with his head against my breast, I lay thinking. Not about my investigation of Leonardo but about sex. Despite my classroom biological knowledge and further readings I'd never grasped its basic characteristic: that it was so *physical.*

As a child, interest in sports was discouraged by my grandmother from fear of injury, and our family's isolation too. Inviting friends to our home had also been discouraged. Not openly but subtly, with looks and shakes of the head that children interpret.

Being self-sufficient I hadn't objected. Feeling content with reading and my grandmother and father and the occasional others in m life. His friends too, cheery to me despite causing anxiety to others.

Huge Rocco bought me boxing gloves and taught me the skill while never landing a blow. And Henry who, with my father's encouragement, taught me to shoot with a revolver in our basement. Using cartridges which contained a primer but no gunpowder enabled us to fire quietly at the target taped to a cardboard box within which the bullets would fall.

Now other realizations arose: of wanting a beloved to share my life and maybe even a child someday. Whether that thought arose from my body or Catholic instruction that the inherent purpose of sex was procreation. I didn't know. Nor was this speculation useful for, as Thomas awoke and faced me, he asked in a not entirely playful tone, "Who are you Miss Whore-In-Training and what's your game?"

Chapter 39

"'Never let a phony take refuge in your head,' my dad told me. Is that what you are?" Thomas asked sadly.

"I am who I said," I replied after a momentary lapse when my mind went blank.

"Really! The simple student who invites herself into a stranger's bed right after meeting him. I don't have movie star looks or money so what's your game?"

When lying keep your story close to the truth is the advice given trainee spies in the novels I'd read so it was what I did.

"Okay, the truth. I am a student though not in economics but at Columbia Law School. And I do like you and wouldn't be here if I didn't. Despite what you think, you are handsome and thoughtful, and sweet which is much more important.

"Two months ago I met Leonardo casually at a restaurant where I hang-out. We've had dinner frequently and I wondered how he is as a boss which is why I contacted you. My slinky dress was the recommended outfit in a novel I read as a teenager. You're my first lover and I don't regret it."

Thomas sat frozen for several moments. Then, without speaking, he lay beside me, took my hand and spoke slowly.

"I hurt you and I'm sorry. Will be see each other again?"

I wasn't sure what to reply. Another phrase from literature burst into my mind: Don't tell your lover how strongly you feel too soon. Was *now* too soon? Had I outgrown only reading about life?

"I want to. Do you?" I asked.

As answer, he leaned over and we began Round Three.

Chapter 40

I couldn't decide whether Thomas or I had become a more accomplished lover but Round Three *was* better. More pleasurable for me and my body was "steaming hot" he said.

They say that all good things must come to an end and this finally did. Dressed in bra, panties, and his bathrobe, we talked over more coffee that night.

"What's your decision about working for Leonardo?" he asked.

"I'm not sure. What you said about being fired for not being a killer makes me uneasy," I said.

"It could have been just his way of saying I'm not aggressive enough. In his defense, he pays well and you'll learn a lot working at his company. I did."

"Maybe."

"Money is important. It gives you independence, the ability to leave on your terms. I didn't have enough but the severance he gave me was outstanding: salary and health insurance for a year. Better than my friends got working for bigger companies."

I said nothing.

"What's your next step?" Thomas asked.

"To continue investigating."

He stared.

"No, not like this. This night wouldn't have happened if I didn't like you and was ready," I said.

"Maybe I can help. I sense that we have different but complementary ways of solving problems. I'm compulsive and detail focused while you make intuitive leaps, seeing connections others can't. I'll be your color coder."

"Huh?" I asked, feeling puzzled.

"We'll classify the LinkedIn people who probably know Leonardo well with different colors: the red ones you contact first, the blue ones you contact next, and the yellow ones you contact if you have more time."

"Sounds like a plan," I said, smiling as I slipped from his robe.

Chapter 41

After leaving Thomas, I tried keeping things light and close to normal. Yet bliss can only last so long in our world as we drift in a sea of ever-changing currents and depths. Change awaits us and can only be embraced, leaving happiness behind.

I had phoned home from his apartment to reduce my grandmother's anxiety. She quickly handed the phone to Roman, likely at his insistence. Though officially our employee, after my father's death he increasingly assumed the role of protective head of family, it being the only family that he ever had.

Though his childhood experiences were brutal, and he was caring toward me to the degree that he was capable. So despite my intention to taxi home, he insisted on driving me. Meeting me at Thomas' apartment and giving him a nod and threatening stare. Each of Roman's encounters with my friends was a gamble, geniality not being one of his skills.

During the drive, though barely leaving Thomas, I felt I couldn't get back to him quickly enough. Finally resigning myself to figuring it out when I got home. Where, thankfully, for once there were no questions.

I felt wide awake and exuberant despite the early hour and having gotten little sleep. Would sex always produce this feeling or only when with Thomas? I certainly liked him but did I love him? Does fate destine women to marry their first love, as in many of my readings? After concluding that time would tell I instantly fell asleep.

Chapter 42

I had expected things to be different after arriving home from my first overnighter but they weren't. Either my grandmother didn't know what to say or decided that not mentioning it was best. Roman seemed the same, only remarking that Thomas was "clean-cut." Which might have been his old-fashioned way of saying "honorable." But I could have been misreading both since their only concern was my well-being.

Despite my slut-outfit, my knowledge of dating etiquette was minimal and I wondered what is expected of a woman next. Online advice provided what seemed sensible tips. She could text him of her safe arrival home or phone to say she had "a good time."

Google's guru added that having similar interests and life goals were major factors in determining if the relationship continued, depending, of course, if your date showed interest in you. And, most importantly, to tell him immediately if you liked him so a "thoughtful second date" could be planned. "In our new world women don't wait," the columnist intoned.

All good advice had our date ended with coffee not wearing his bathrobe but is sex so important nowadays? While considering this, I remembered a conversation that I overheard in the Columbia University Library. "I went to his room wearing only a raincoat," one girl said. "My first question when I go to a boy's room is if the door is locked," said another. "I carry condoms on every date. A six-pack to be sure," the third girl said casually and all laughed.

It really is a new world, I decided.

Chapter 43

I hadn't needed to decide what to do next since, as I sat sleepy-eyed after studying corporate law, Thomas phoned me.

"What are you doing today?" he asked in an engaging tone.

"Studying," I said, not wanting to seem too easy.

"And thinking about me too I hope," he said.

"Okay, that too," I admitted, with a giggle that escaped.

"While doing my job search I worked on yours. Cross-referenced from LinkedIn a list of Leonardo's former workers for you to interview."

"That's sweet of you."

"You might speak with the disgruntled ones first, to learn what dirt they have if any."

"Your idea of color-coding them by importance..." I began but he interrupted.

"Already done."

"You're a brick. I owe you," I said.

"Come over. You can pick it up," he said.

I hesitated, knowing that sex was what he had in mind. Not wanting to appear easy to get though being as ready as him.

"An early dinner would be fine. Is 5:00PM Okay?"

My grandmother, who had been quietly knitting opposite me, now spoke. "I'd like to meet your young man."

This'll keep it kosher, I thought.

"My grandmother wants to meet you. She'll come too," I said.

"I'd love to meet her," Thomas said, after a long pause.

"Okay. How about ABCV on East 19th Street? We're both into healthy eating."

"I'll be there."

"We've got a date," I told my grandmother.

She smiled.

Chapter 44

"We must dress properly," was my grandmother's injunction, in her subtle criticism of the slut costume that I wore to my date with Thomas. Hers was a green print shirtwaister dress of vintage 1950s style. Mine was a black crepe long sleeve which extended below the knee.

Roman took pains too, wearing what might be regarded as a chauffeur's uniform complete with cap. Before leaving my grandmother nodded approval of all. While being driven to the restaurant I felt like a princess, ignoring their fate in so many fairy tales.

Thomas had taken pains with his appearance too, wearing an obviously expensive blue plaid jacket, open-necked light blue shirt, and matching slacks.

After a brief introduction at the door, we went to our reserved table. The restaurant was bright and airy with a relaxing nature vibe. The fact that it wasn't crowded despite having outstanding reviews aroused the thought that I had chosen a good time.

I ordered quickly for all, as if to get this necessity out of the way. Green chickpea hummus with whole wheat pita, spinach spaghetti with broccoli and kale, whole roasted cauliflower with herbs and pistachio. For beverage, I and my grandmother had iced tea and Thomas had rosewater lemonade. Tasty food though discussion was the major goal of all. While awaiting the food, my grandmother faced Thomas.

"How did you meet my granddaughter?" she asked.

"It was she who met me, seeking my advice," Thomas said smoothly.

This evening might not be as bad as I feared, I thought.

Chapter 45

The evening *was* better.

"My granddaughter is an accomplished woman. I and my son gave her a good upbringing," my grandmother said.

Her statement might have led to so many questions that I feared Thomas' response but he handled the situation smoothly.

"She is," he merely said, and the rest of the conversation concerned the restaurant's food and decor.

But you can only spend so much time on such topics so, forty-minutes later, my grandmother was being driven home, satisfied that she'd done her duty.

"She's sweet," Thomas said after she left.

"You're seeing her at her best. She hungers for a grandchild and was assessing your potential," I said.

"What do you think she decided?" Thomas asked.

"Well, you're certainly a catch, being educated and attractive. We could make good babies when I'm ready but which won't be for some time. I'm still a student, remember."

"And more."

"And more," I agreed with a smile. "Now let's see what you put together."

His list included twenty-three names, listed in order of who he considered to have the most valuable information.

"That's a lot of people," I said.

"You needn't contact all. Stop when you feel you've learned enough. None are current employees. Speaking with them would be too risky."

I was glad he didn't say the obvious: his hope I didn't believe that information could only be gained through sex. But he seemed to read my mind.

"You could make impressive credentials with a printer and virtual office rental."

"You're clever. My dad would have liked you too," I blurted, instantly blushing at the thought of my father's murder-for-hire career.

But Thomas only smiled.

Chapter 46

I peered at the list as if studying each name though my thinking was elsewhere. Before leaving the restaurant my grandmother said I should phone when Roman should return for me. Her loud voice caused a nearby couple to look our way and her message was clear: my approval of Thomas doesn't mean I believe you grown-up enough to have an affair. Which I also felt might be right. Before making an awkward remark, Thomas decided for me.

"I must leave early. My mother is visiting from Columbus and I'll be meeting her at the airport," he said.

The change to a "safe" topic calmed me.

"What's your mother like?" I asked.

"What is she like?" Thomas said rhetorically. "You'll like her as most people do. Congenial to others but too narcissistic to be the good mother kids deserve."

I smiled agreeably until his shocking statement.

"She tried to abort me."

All emotion drained from my face. Just like Leonardo and me, Thomas' childhood had been weird. Isn't any parent normal? I thought.

"How do you know? That's not something a mother tells their child," I said.

"Of course she didn't. I heard it from an older cousin who knows family gossip. Both our mothers tried to abort us using physical activity, jumping from a stepladder while holding a heavy container. I was born three months prematurely and survived in an incubator. After birth my mother took me to doctors continually, probably from guilt and the fear that there was something wrong with me. Finally, when I was about five, I remember the doctor saying, "Leave your boy alone. He's perfectly healthy," and she did. It's too bad that what he meant wasn't emotionally."

Dead To Life

"Wow!" I said.
It was enough.

Chapter 47

"How did you feel after hearing Thomas' story?" Doctor Hess had asked.

"Shocked but also nothing. Like leaving the theater for a snack after being terrified by a horror movie," I replied.

"What shocked you? His mother's attempted abortion or Thomas speaking casually of it?"

"Both, I guess. Abortion should be the decision of a woman and her doctor but done medically. Not by jumping off a stepladder."

"What's the difference?"

"What his mother did might have caused Thomas to be born brain damaged or whatever."

"I'm not expressing a moral judgment on abortion but to abort is to kill," Doctor Hess said.

"To kill..."

"Did you know your father's business as a child."

The long silence that followed was broken by another question.

"What are you thinking?"

"When I was about five I was awoken by the sound of my parents arguing. "I know," my father said.

"You know what?" my mother asked.

"About all your friends as you call them. My Swedish whore, the mother of my child."

"Yes, I'm her mother but are you really her father? Does her good intelligence really run in your family's genes? How many became doctors or lawyers? How many rose from the gutter?"

"We live well," my father said calmly.

"Yes, but I know where the money comes from and what you do."

Once again I became silent.

"What did your father reply?" Doctor Hess had asked.

"He didn't."

"How long after that conversation did your mother disappear?"

"A month later," I said.

Chapter 48

Because the restaurant had become crowded and noisy, we went to Thomas' apartment to study the list he created. There, my clothes stayed on and Thomas didn't comment. Roger was the first name on the list.

"Why did you place him first?" I asked.

"He worked for Leonardo for ten years. Leaving after being mugged so seriously that it made the news. His left arm was shattered and he was shot in the knee. What made it stranger was that nothing was stolen. Not even his eleven-thousand-dollar gold Cartier watch."

"Like it was done to send a lesson," I said.

"That's what I and others thought but it wasn't in the article. I did some checking."

"Huh?"

"With a high school friend that owes me. My dad pulled strings and got him released without being charged after being picked up for smoking pot. He's now a detective at a midtown precinct."

"What did he find?"

"It was the absence of motive that made the assault 'interesting' as he phrased it, not what you'd expect. No raging spouse or girlfriend, no gambling debt, no revenge-seeking relative. His life was untroubled except for one thing: that he left his last job on bad terms, suing it for what he considered was unpaid compensation due him."

"And the company was?"

"Leonardo's."

"I see why he's first on your list. I should speak with him," I said.

"You will. I've invited him for brunch on Saturday. There's more to the story. Before the assault came Helter-Skelter. But I'll let him tell you about it," Thomas said.

Dead To Life

I gasped, knowing what Helter-Skelter was.

Chapter 49

For most people "helter-skelter" is an adverb meaning to behave in a hurried confused manner without definite purpose. But readers of crime novels knew its historic roots both as song and association with a notorious blood-soaked crime.

"Helter Skelter" is a song by "The Beatles," an English rock band in what became known as their White Album. It was their attempt to create a sound as loud as possible and a key influence in the development of heavy metal. Along with other album tracks it was interpreted by a California cult leader, Charles Manson, as a message predicting interracial war after which only Manson followers would survive.

In 1969, Manson and several followers went to six Los Angeles homes, killing the residents who included the actress Sharon Tate. The word "Pig," "Helter Skelter, "Rise," and "Death to Pigs" was written on furniture.

"Where will we meet Roger?" I asked calmly despite my raging brain.

"I made a reservation at Narcisse. It's not far from here on Second Avenue."

I didn't reply, my mind still fixed on helter-skelter. It seemed to symbolize what I'd experienced in the media storm at the time of my father's execution. Thomas continued, misreading my discomfort and believing it related to the restaurant's menu.

"Narcisse has a broad menu and I chose it because of your vegetarian leanings. You can get French Toast or salad or omelet. Its gotten great reviews."

"I'm sure it'll be OK. I'd better leave, get to bed early," I said.

Then, after a chaste kiss, I did.

Chapter 50

The words "helter-skelter" must have troubled me more than I realized since I slept little that night. Next morning I told my grandmother of my brunch engagement and she didn't object. Having met Thomas had apparently increased her trust in my judgment. Despite this she had Roman accompany me and I didn't object. His pistol was a better safety precaution than my stun Poison-Pen.

"Why are you meeting these men?" he asked in the car.

"I'm trying to get inside information from former disgruntled workers about a job I might take," I said.

"You don't need the money. Why take it at all?" he asked.

That's a good question I thought.

"I have too much energy to sit home doing nothing or aimless travel around the world. My brain needs activity. I'll molder without it," I said. Not adding that the life of a non-working wife wasn't for me.

"I understand. Your father couldn't stand being idle. He always kept busy," Roman said.

This was a part of my father that I didn't know.

"What did he do?" I asked.

Roman hesitated for so long that I felt he wouldn't answer. When he did I understood why and his information stunned me.

"He loved to read and when not reading he wrote his autobiography," he said.

"I knew about the reading but not that," I said.

"He never said but I think he intended his writing for you."

"I want to read it. Where is it?" I asked.

"It was given me for safekeeping. I'll bring it to you." Roman said.

Dead To Life

We spoke no more during the remainder of the drive. It was my father's writings and not helter-skelter which occupied my mind as we entered the restaurant.

Chapter 51

Narcisse's airy quiet atmosphere was a good choice for a discussion, I thought. Thomas and Roger arrived early. Upon seeing Roman, Thomas invited him to join us. After glancing toward me he did and was introduced as my driver.

Roger was a balding thin man in his forties with bags under his eyes that made him seem older. His left arm moved stiffly, likely from the wound that he suffered during the mugging I thought. His occasional wince from pain might be a residue of the bullet he took to the knee.

The waiter approached and we ordered: French Toast for me with a side order of Roasted Carrots for nutrition; Eggs Florentine (eggs on a bed of spinach with hollandaise sauce) for Thomas; and Steak and Eggs for Roger. Just the sight of meat can cause my vegetarian stomach to do flips but I kept it in check. Roman followed our discussion while sticking with coffee, considering himself on-duty.

As soon as the waiter left, Thomas introduced me as the business reporter for a start-up subscription business publication, one that paid for interviews in more than publicity. For today's interview Roger would be paid two-thousand-five-hundred-dollars with future payment if another interview was needed. The possibility of a lucrative management job was also dangled. Roger's eyes widened at this offer particularly since the publishing industry isn't known for largesse.

"What was your experience with Leonardo?" I asked Roger.

"Wonderful for much of the time. He's brilliant and I learned a lot from him. We even had him over my house for dinner and my kids loved him. My five-year-old daughter called him 'my buddy.' Things only changed later, when I started asking questions."

"What did you question?" I asked.

"Record entries of odd payments that made no sense to companies that seemed to exist only as post-office boxes. Things got worse when I demanded what I considered was owed me."

The food arrived and we began eating. "Good," he remarked of the food before continuing.

"Thomas said he told you of my mugging during which nothing was stolen but I was beaten and shot. *Kneecapped* as IRA terrorists did to traitors. That scared me but much worse was the helter-skelter.

"While I was in the hospital, my wife and kids stayed with her parents in Rye. Two days later when I returned home I found the furnishings rearranged, and not by my wife. You know how you become sure how objects in a room are. Now several pictures were hung on different walls and scatter rugs were moved, the same with where my toothbrush and razor are usually placed. But nothing was destroyed so police would take it seriously or you'd even feel comfortable calling them from fear of being thought crazy."

"You'd been sent a message," Roman said and Roger looked at him sharply.

"Yes. That they can get to me anytime."

Chapter 52

Returning to my role of business reporter, I asked, "What have you told your wife?"

"Nothing of the truth. What can I say? That I was an idiot who ignored the facts until too late. That any day we might be murdered depending on the whim of a man who our son calls 'buddy'?"

Roman's face darkened as Roger spoke. Perhaps it was the speaking of family that did it. My grandmother told me that, like with many abused children, family was a sacred notion to him.

"Isn't your remedy obvious?" he asked Roger, who didn't respond and Roman continued.

"An ancient Chinese saying is, 'Dangerous enemies will meet again in narrow streets,' and a German proverb, 'He who has three enemies must agree with two.' To avoid having to continually look over your shoulder you must ally yourself with Leonardo's enemies and become an army."

"Not exactly the Biblical advice of praying for those who mistreat you," Thomas said, with a small smile.

"Not unless you want to be eaten by a lion," Roman replied, returning attention to his coffee as if intending to speak no more.

"Has Leonardo other enemies who share your concerns about his funds?"

"Just rumors I've heard. One is of a partner who died by suicide. Shooting himself with an old pistol whose serial number had been erased, an odd weapon for anyone but a crook to have. I would have thought he'd have bought a new gun wouldn't you?"

Our unspoken agreement hung in the air.

Chapter 53

"What do you plan to do now?" I asked Roger.

"What do I plan to do?" he repeated rhetorically. "I intend to spend time healing while deciding. Thankfully my wife is a lawyer so we won't starve or be homeless. Though unfortunately as a public defender and not at a lucrative private firm. Then I could retire to stay-at-home dad."

Conversation petered out and attention returned to our food.

"You won't identify me in your article will you?" Roger asked.

My response was slow in coming as I needed re-enter my reporter role.

"No. What you told me will only be used as background. Nor will Leonardo be mentioned. Doing that would be legally risky."

We finished our coffees, the meal ended, and I rose to leave. Can I give you a lift?" I asked Roger.

"Thanks. I was going to take a taxi but it can be hard getting one at this time," he said.

I hadn't planned to make this offer and didn't know why I did. Roman seemed surprised too. It might have been Roger's obvious discomfort as he walked.

His apartment, on Manhattan's Upper East Side, wasn't far. Upon reaching his building I accepted his invitation to meet his family. Roman sought a parking space after saying that I should phone before leaving.

Roger's wife, Cindy, was a tall thin blond in her early thirties, the trophy wife that any hedge fund manager would want added to her professional degree. Their two children, five and three, had his wife's complexion and the relaxed attitude of neither.

She stared with a puzzled expression as he introduced me.

"You look familiar," she said.

While trying to keep calm I reminded myself that I now looked far different from the fourteen-year-old media celebrity I once was.

"I've been told I have a generic pretty face," I said casually.

"*Pretty face*," their five-year-old daughter exclaimed.

Our laughs ended the tense moment.

"Yesterday, when our au pair asked her to hurry up in the bathroom, she said, "I am but it takes me a long time to wipe my butt."

We all laughed again.

"I liked the family," I had told Doctor Hess.

Chapter 54

"What did you like about Roger's family?" Doctor Hess had asked.

"I'm not sure. Maybe because it seemed so different from mine."

"How so?"

"I didn't consider mine different when I was a kid even though I had sleepovers at their homes but none at mine. They didn't visit my home either but I didn't consider this strange. My grandmother and parents liked it quiet so I thought it was because of that and gloomy Roman being always around."

"When did you start sensing the difference?" he asked.

"Really only after his arrest when everything changed. I was removed from school to be home-schooled and hid in my room with the blinds drawn. Reading sci-fi novels about alien invasion enthralled me. Maybe because it was like what was happening, an alien invasion into my family which changed everything and caused unimaginable terror. You can't imagine what it's like having a camera thrust into your face wherever you go."

"It must have been horrifying. What did your grandmother tell you?" he asked.

"Nothing to really explained it. She said my father was mistakenly arrested. That it was an adult matter to be dealt with by adults and my job as a child was to study. That she and Roman would deal with everything else."

"Did you believe her?"

"I accepted rather than believed and tried to ignore. What could a teenager do? And my period had just started so I had enough to puzzle over. Finding a female gynecologist, which I insisted, wasn't easy but my grandmother eventually did."

The silence that followed was ended by his question.

"Would you have preferred a female analyst?"

"That didn't occur to me and I thought most were men. Seeing you feels comfortable." I said.

"All people have both male and female psychological characteristics. Some men are more maternal and the mothering figure in the family toward their children, and some woman are more vocationally aggressive which is considered a male trait. The sex of the therapist rarely matters except possibly when a woman was abused by her father."

"My father was the loving parent," I said.

"So it seems," Doctor Hess said.

Chapter 55

I didn't spend that night with Thomas or the next. Not because, having met him, my grandmother would have objected but because I'd changed. Adopting the identity of a business reporter had seemed to cause this. Or maybe it was because I had now become fully sexual which is a big event, to have a man value your body and call it beautiful as Thomas had done.

I was grateful to him for enabling my development but didn't know if I loved him. Would I want to marry and spend my entire life with him, which the remnant of my Catholic upbringing mandates? No, or at least not yet.

Being a novice investigator I puzzled over what should come next: to interview more people or study Leonardo more closely. Being unable to decide, I took a bath during which a brainstorm hit: I would become Leonardo's *daughter*.

Not his real daughter, which is impossible, but one who would *seem* real which would take more than a little acting. But would this really be hard? I asked myself, since I had been acting all my life, Fantasizing myself the beloved heroine of novels, the woman enraptured by love and life. And perhaps gaining sanity too, having always felt myself more than a little crazy.

Achieving this would require me to groom Leonardo as my father, similarly to how a sex abuser groomed their prey. Not the most comfortable analogy but, as I said, I read many novels and was a bit crazy too.

Chapter 56

Having lived inside my fantasy imaginative bubble since childhood and not knowing where to begin, I turned to Google to learn how predators operate despite my uncertainty whether the information was accurate.

There, seduction was described as a performance act depending on the nature of the relationship. That the seducer had to know who they would be speaking to whether child or adult, rich or struggling. And, most importantly, their ambition, it being a struggle until learning that.

Next is creating a dependence by asking questions. Whether their mother is alright or, if a parent with their child, whether they'd like to hold your puppy's leash for a moment. This initial bonding, whether real or artificial, opens discussion and establishes dependence on the seducer, which is the first step toward being betrayed. That in every relationship there is the dupe and the string- puller, the person being controlled and the one in control, who is what I planned to be.

I constructed my psychological portrait of Leonardo. He was elderly, wealthy, and lonely. Having no wife or children which, also according to Google, are increasingly longed for as one ages. Why else would he spend so many evenings with me, a young woman whose friendship could gain him no worldly advantage.

Nor did he desire my body since he'd never made a romantic advance and could afford the most desirable prostitute. Not that romancing me would had succeeded because of the age difference and my financial independence.

Thus was created the nature of my performance. I would be the loving, needful child he desired.

Chapter 57

Beginning my performance with Leonardo wasn't difficult since it merely comprised continuing our activities as they'd been. Studying evenings at the restaurant's corner table until he appeared at the stroke of seven before we ordered, and for which he insisted on paying as a parent always does for their young child.

A thought entered my mind while waiting and reading a paper from that day's legal ethics class about lawyers who swindle their clients.

After pressuring by state legislatures, the legal profession has tried to remedy the actions of its disreputable members. The first system of reimbursement was established in Vermont in 1958, to be paid by lawyers' dues.

Most of the offenders, many of whom were gamblers, alcoholics, or drug addicts, graduated from marginal law schools and made their living by cheating vulnerable clients. As Mario Cuomo, the lawyer who became New York's governor remarked, "Even in a barrel of New York's finest, there's bound to be a bad apple or two." Several of the cases that I read are heartbreaking.

One lawyer stole $167,000 in pension money from a widow recovering from a nervous breakdown following the death of her husband on Christmas. Another lawyer not only stole $71,000 from an elderly client but also her piano. A father-and-son legal team stole $75,000 from a child who was orphaned after his sister arranged to murder their parents, and $150,000 from an estate bequeathing this sum to an organization training Seeing Eye dogs. Surpassing these crooks was the Connecticut probate judge accused of stealing three-million-dollars from his clients.

Stunned by these examples, I remembered what my father casually told me: "A lawyer can steal more with their pen than a bank robber with a gun."

Dead To Life

"What are you reading?" Leonardo asked, as he sat opposite me.

Chapter 58

"An ethics class paper about lawyers who steal," I said.

"A lawyer can steal more with a pen than a robber with a gun," Leonardo said.

I stared openmouthed.

"What? You never heard that?"

"Years ago my father said exactly that," I said.

"It was said by the legendary bank robber Willie Sutton," he said, and described his exploits.

"Sutton was one of the most successful bank robbers in history, famed for his daring thefts, ability to evade police, and charm. He was a master planner who avoided using force to gain success.

"His key strength was the research he did preparing for robberies. Identifying weaknesses in the bank's security and gaining information about its employees' routines to avoid surprise.

"He used disguises and deception, wearing a false beard or eyeglasses, and tricking employees to gain access to the vault as by saying he was a maintenance worker.

"He and worked with a team, assigning each member specific responsibilities and using code words and signals to avoid police detection. He was also flexible, knowing that things don't always go according to plan and prepared to adjust his strategy like if there was a change of bank guards. This ability to think on his feet and adapt to changing circumstances enabled his successes.

"Most of all, he wasn't reckless. He minimized risk by choosing his targets carefully, those without high security measures or strong police presence.

"An entrepreneur can gain valuable lessons from his life: the importance of research, teamwork, preparation, and flexibility in gaining success.

"Still, there's an unfortunate corollary to Sutton's life. After his last of several escapes from prison, he was recognized on a subway and followed by twenty-four-year-old Arnold Schuster, a Brooklyn clothing salesman and amateur detective who reported him to the police. After appearing on TV, Schuster was murdered by order of a Mafia boss who disliked Schuster for being 'a rat' and ' squealer.'"

I took mental notes from Leonardo's soliloquy, believing that in speaking of Sutton he was also speaking of himself. But I couldn't help wondering: Is his description of squealer Schuster's murder intended as warning to me?

Chapter 59

I slept poorly that night, being awakened just after midnight by my frequent nightmare of having to *see* something though feeling it would destroy me. Lying paralyzed beneath the covers, I wondered what it could be.

The secret might be of a family matter: my mother's disappearance or my father's fearsome vocation. But these were known: my mother left our family to live with a lover and my father had been a hired killer. I would likely never fully adjust to my mother's absence since no child can accept their mother's willing desertion. Easier to accept that my father murdered her.

It was surprisingly easy to accept that my father had been a murderer. Maybe because all of his victims had deserved the common fate of criminals who ordered the death of others. One might say that my father was carrying out the wishes of Heaven.

"You don't really believe that do you?" Doctor Hess had asked when I said this.

"I sometimes do. How else could I let myself continue loving him?" I asked.

"You're discovering the power of the unconscious," Doctor Hess said approvingly.

"I'd sooner have been blessed with a conventional family. Though my father loved me and provided for me after he was gone."

"Yes to both," Doctor Hess said.

"Has there been any change in your recurring nightmare?" he asked a minute later.

"None except that it feels more terrifying. I seem to be moving closer to the sight that will destroy me if I see it."

"No dream, no matter how horrifying, can hurt in real life."

Dead To Life

"No, but what happens in life certainly can."

Chapter 60

What happened next day *did* terrify me even though it was just an Apple News item. A civil rights organization opposed to capital punishment had sued to gain access to execution audios of Virginia's death chamber, of which existence it had just learned. I couldn't keep myself from reading the gory details which were far more horrifying than the execution I witnessed. Afterward, all that day, I anxiously spoke with the babbling-brook urgency of a person starved for comfort.

Before my father's execution I walked within a small group through the prison yard to the squat brick building containing the death chamber. The building had windowless doors permitting different groups of witnesses to avoid each other, those present for the condemned and others for their victims.

When the black curtains opened I saw what resembled an operating room with tile walls. My father looked from window to window, hoping to see me or so I thought. He had not asked that I stay away. At 8:00AM he said, "I'm sorry for the grief and pain I've caused." Then, after a brief telephone call to learn if clemency had been granted, the warden said, "Proceed with the execution."

Though having spoken calmly, my father's feet moved nervously as the drugs that stopped lungs flowed into him through tubes stretching from a far wall. He blinked a few times and died with his eyes open, the whole process taking perhaps four minutes.

When the curtains in our witness room closed, we silently left the building. While seated in the car with my eyes tightly shut, I tried not to hear the reporters' screaming questions as we left the prison yard on the long ride home.

Chapter 61

As my investigation of Leonardo progressed, our relationship changed. Though still dining at the restaurant, this having become almost a ritual, he now shared more of his life.

After numerous failed relationships, he turned to work for joy in life. His employees had become his family, containing the intense emotions of typical families.

"Workers bring childhood troubles to their job," he told me, not realizing how true this was of him.

With this change I shared more too, speaking of my life-long loneliness strengthened by living in a family of secrets, and my solitary nature. Of my yearning for my loving, lost father and the loving mother I never had within my current family of grandmother and bodyguard.

"Could this be why you considered working for Leonardo?" Doctor Hess had asked.

"Partly, but I think it was also my father's attitude, how he related to the world. Not with blind sadism but as a business necessity with as little pain as possible. I once read that despite the horror of Soviet rule, its executions were conducted morally and without excruciating delay. Without notice, the condemned would be asked to stand on a line and an officer would shoot him in back of the head. Kinder than what happens in America," I said.

"What did Leonardo say about your father?" Doctor Hess asked.

"Just that he seemed to have loved me," I said.

Chapter 62

Leonardo's summary of my father's life, that despite his misdeeds he had loved me, marked a change in our relationship. I lost interest in investigating him and sought to know him instead. Both as a person and, though I didn't immediately sense this, as a *real* replacement for the father I lost.

Not as a parent who would tell me what to do, try to control me, but as a listener to my lonesome self. Providing honest opinions on such matters as my career, and whether I was ready to settle down with a man and Thomas in particular. This, despite the negative employee judgment that Leonardo had made of him.

"How much of this indicated your emotional needs and how much Leonardo's grooming of you?" Doctor Hess had asked.

"Probably both. During every seduction the target hungers for what's being offered. A prospective worker to be hired, the horny for a sex partner, and this lonesome dove for a father and a friend," I said.

"All true, but do you recognize how often you put yourself down. How many could have survived a life like yours: one who lacked a real mother, could demand to be present at their father's execution, and investigate a powerful figure. You're a survivor!"

I didn't argue. Doctor Hess was a renowned psychoanalyst and he charged an impressive fee.

Chapter 63

"What are you thinking?" Doctor Hess finally asked after my long silence.

"About what you said, why I was so open to being seduced by Leonardo. Thinking that it indicated more than his skill and my need for another father."

"What do you think it was?"

"My hunger for success like his, to become a respected person unlike my father. Who, despite what people said of him, was just trying to survive. You called me a survivor and he was a survivor too."

"By killing people?" Doctor Hess asked.

Rage poured through me at his sneering tone and I almost jumped from my seat.

"Let's compare your life to his," I said deliberately. "Both your parents were doctors and you grew up in a ritzy town in Alabama. Maybe related to a German rocket scientist recruited by America after the war, prospering from the melted gold teeth of concentration camp victims banked in Switzerland. Maybe made into the gold ring you wear."

Doctor Hess's smile made me even angrier.

"What's funny you Nazi pig?" I screamed.

"Nothing you said. I'm just pleased you've finally expressed the rage you've buried so long. Factually, my father was an Army doctor and my mother a Jewish nurse. Which makes *me* Jewish according to its tradition.

"In Biblical times the child's religion was passed through the father and not the mother but because of intermarriage with members of other tribes the religious lineage was changed to the mother. There was no DNA testing then and you could tell who the mother was. Still, my family was stationed in Germany for years and I speak German fluently so there's *some* truth to what you said. Not much but some," he said with a small smile.

"I'm sorry," I said contritely, as my face reddened.

"Don't be. Your feelings are finally bursting through, which is the essential precursor to change."

Chapter 64

Before beginning my psychoanalytic treatment I asked myself whether it was even possible to bring order out of the memories bustling through my thoughts. The traumatizing ones from my father's execution would invade even the most benign, like decisions about study and how my body felt with Thomas.

"You were traumatized, which is just being human," Doctor Hess said when I spoke of this worry. "The mind has a certain tolerance for stress that, when exceeded, creates symptoms which are the sign that something is wrong."

"There's been a lot wrong with my life," I said.

To which summary statement Doctor Hess simply nodded.

I've already described my father's execution, my years at Barnard and Columbia Law School, and the meals with Leonardo but not how I changed under his tutelage. Having always been an accomplished student I now became his. Gaining new abilities though his lessons weren't extraordinary. Not the financial shenanigans that I later learned but those critical to all business success and not only in crime. Which, as he said, "is business on steroids."

"I was a weary starving prospector until finding a speck of gold on the heel of my boot. Lifting the speck with the tip of my knife and staring as it grew in my imagination from a tiny grain to a nugget and then to a fabulous stake. These specks of gold are what I'm giving you," he said.

Many instructive stories followed such portentous words. Slowly, from my role as beginner seated before an adept. Some examples were difficult to grasp, causing me to feel like the bold beginning explorer who finds their trail increasingly rough and narrow until dwindling into rock-studded hills or a morass of mud.

Dead To Life

"Wars have been fought since Carthage. Life is a series of wars," Leonardo said, at the end of one meal.

"Did you believe him?" Doctor Hess asked.

"How could I not? My father was killed," I said.

Chapter 65

That a child hangs onto hope long after hope has expired has always seemed a truism for me. Even if it is one so absurd as that my father still lived though having viewed his execution. Which seemed as if it were a drama, as the witnesses almost think. That all were actors in a poorly written horror show, knowing this was not true but feeling it could be.

In my later dreams, not the one of the frightening sight awaiting me, my father stood tall and healthy. Telling me, as I lay in his outstretched arms, that I was smart and beautiful, a woman no husband would fully deserve. What father could say more? What daughter wanted less?

This, Leonardo seemed to understand and what I felt he yearned to provide. To be my father and I his beloved child. He would be my teacher, as every father is, and I would learn, as the dutiful child I had always been.

I still don't know if our bonding reflected reality or shared unrealizable yearnings. That my father would again live, and Leonardo's hunger for a child be satisfied. But in the end it didn't matter. He had his need and I had mine. I grew to love him and I think he loved me. Then, the notion of betrayal had drifted far from my mind.

At graduation I ranked second in my law school class. I really ranked first but having the daughter of an executed murderer give the valedictory speech would have been unthinkable even for our progressive administrators. So, rather than attend that ceremony, Leonardo created our own. At his home where I met his latest "best friend," Ingrid. A long-legged Swede, she was younger than me and had a striking resemblance to the mother who deserted me.

Chapter 66

Though Ingrid might not have been her real name, she was sweet and attentive to guests. Like the ideal housewife of daytime TV shows and I liked her. Leonardo related to her as husbands do, if the romance novels that I read were accurate. My presence as his acolyte daughter completed the picture of this otherwise childless couple. A totally safe relationship, one to be easily discarded by the wary "husband."

Seeming to recognize my special relationship with Leonardo or perhaps following his signal, Ingrid continually attended other guests, leaving Leonardo and I alone. It was during one of these moments that Leonardo made his offer.

"Hardly anyone gets to be in movies but with me you can be in adventures they make movies about," he whispered, as New York City's Mayor approached.   "What did you say?" Doctor Hess had asked.

"Nothing. I just nodded acceptance," I said.

Though termed a casual affair, all of the men wore suits and ties and the women's clothes were equally studied. None would have dared wear the current near-naked attire. Their personalities were equally similar, driven by anger and the hunger for power overlain with charm.

While observing the scene from a corner, Ingrid approached with a broad smile. "You're beautiful and they're staring. Don't be alone with any man here," she whispered.

I opened my purse to her view. It held a small Springfield Armory 9MM pistol and a more terrifying Fox Folding Knife. Obtaining my carry pistol permit requires political favor in this gun phobic city but the knife is available on the internet.

I returned her smile. "Thank you for your concern but I'm not afraid. I'd Bobbitt them," I said, telling her of Lorena Bobbitt who became a public figure after slicing off her husband's penis in 1993. She later evolved into an advocate for survivors of domestic violence with her name becoming a noun for what could happen.

Though initially startled, Ingrid quickly relaxed and touched my hand.

"We'll be good friends," she said.

Chapter 67

My comment seemed to cement our sisterhood and we stood close for the rest of the evening.

"How did you meet Leonardo?" I asked.

"At a business meeting in Stockholm, exchanging comments at a finance seminar. I have a degree from the London School of Economics." Adding, as my face registered surprise, "I'm not a simple whore."

"I didn't think you were. Not with Leonardo," I said.

"He's an unusual man. How are you related?" she asked.

"We're not. While a law student we met while sharing a restaurant table. He's interested in the law and I in business," I said.

During the silence that followed Ingrid studied my face.

"You're *her*, a media sensation even in Sweden. The American girl who insisted on witnessing her father's execution."

Whether from my increased maturity or the remark's frequency this recognition no longer infuriated me.

"That's me," I said simply.

"How could you watch the horror?" she burst out, deeply troubled.

"I loved him. People do painful things for love. Maybe that's why I could never let myself love again," I said.

"Even in sleep, unforgotten pain drops on our heart. Leonardo likes me because I'm smart. He may even love me," she said, becoming tearful.

"We *will* be friends," I said.

"I hope so. I can use one," she said.

"You must meet a lot of people at his soirees," I said.

"So that's that they're called," she said with a smile. "I always thought of them as shooting galleries, the hunter and his pigeons."

"Where would you place me?" I asked, feeling visibly shaken, this conversation not being what I expected.

"This is your party. Maybe the cook."

Neither of us smiled.

"Let's get away from here. We can talk in Leonardo's office," she said.

Chapter 68

What Ingrid termed Leonardo's office wasn't what I expected though considering his achievements I shouldn't have expected less. Just as I had been surprised by his tie's yellow, black and green stripes which belonged to some English regiment.

The office featured an Italian Renaissance chandelier, a huge fireplace, rich red woodwork with glass enclosed bookcases containing books chosen for reading rather than by decorator for color, paneled walls, and a Dutch door, a horizontally divided door so the upper part can be opened while the lower part stays closed, leading onto the garden. The well-carved desk with multiple drawers might have been used by President Theodore Roosevelt. While comfortably sprawled on a large gray sofa, Ingrid told me her shocking tale, but one that I sensed was entirely true.

"How old were you when you first had sex?" she asked.

I said nothing, feeling both surprise and shock.

"I'm asking for a reason. It's not a seduction," she said reassuringly.

"I didn't think it was. I just felt surprised and maybe a little ashamed. I first had sex two months ago. Pretty old, huh?"

"There's no rule. I first had sex at thirteen."

"They start early in Sweden," I said.

"No more than elsewhere. It was with my sixteen-year-old brother," Ingrid said.

I didn't reply immediately, not knowing what to say. Talking about sex isn't easy for Catholics even today.

"Did your mother know?" I asked finally.

"Of course. She knew everything going on in the family. But ignored it like she did everything unpleasant."

"How long did it last, between you and your brother?" I asked.

"Four years but not all the time since he was away at school much of the time. We lived on Oland, the second largest Swedish island, connected to the mainland by a three-mile bridge. Craziness seems to develop easily in isolated areas. My father was a county official and my mother spent her time cleaning the house. Both died young from lung cancer. They were heavy smokers."

"What's your brother doing now?" I asked.

"I don't know. I tried to avoid him when he was home during school vacations and we didn't speak during my parents' funerals."

Chapter 69

"I had a dream last night," Ingrid said, after a long silence.

"Did you tell it to Leonardo?" I asked.

" Our relationship isn't like that but you'll understand. We're both damaged goods."

"We are," I agreed.

"In my dream, I was walking in a city, trying to get somewhere it was important for me to be but I don't know why. I believed the area was dangerous and became terrified when I saw teenagers standing around but passed them unmolested as they sang of friendship and togetherness. I kept walking and found myself lost in a tenement, having a hard time finding my way out but finally doing so. When I left the building I remembered that I had a dog at home that I'd left uncared for. She'd grown thin from lack of food and water and care and I felt tremendous guilt about this. What could my dream mean?" she asked with tear-filled eyes.

"What did you tell her?" Doctor Hess had asked.

"At first I wasn't sure I should say anything. What if what I said sent her crashing. Then a thought hit me: that what her dream symbolized also applied to me. So I did tell her.

"Two things hit me about your dream: that you feel the world is dangerous, which is false, and that you haven't been taking care of yourself, the wasted-away puppy symbolizing you."

"How did she react to your interpretation?" Doctor Hess asked.

"At first she didn't say anything. Then she jumped up and hugged me," I said.

Chapter 70

"You've really suffered," I said.

"So have you," Ingrid said.

"Not like you. My mother left us but my father loved me. He would have killed anyone that hurt me," I said, and she looked up sharply.

"Considering your father's profession that probably wasn't the best choice of words," she said, and we shared a smile.

"Did you ever want to kill him, your brother?" I asked, unable to stifle my curiosity.

"Growing up in a crazy family causes you to feel beaten-down, without exit except hopefully when you're older. How about you?"

"Only the reporters who hounded me during my media stardom. And killing always seemed theoretical to me despite what's written about my father," I said.

"Is what they wrote true?" she asked.

"I don't think about it. How could I? He loved me and I loved him which is why I wanted to be with him until the end."

Silence enveloped us until Ingrid said, "I had another dream last night. In it I was trying to rescue a policeman that was attacked but my effort wound up getting him killed."

"How did you interpret that dream?" Doctor Hess had asked.

"I couldn't but it stuck in my mind. Despite you saying that dreams don't predict, in view of what later happened."

Chapter 71

The graduation party seemed more a political event with its guests of judges, politicians, and fat-cat donors. Ingrid separated from my side as we left Leonardo's office, she being its official hostess.

Gliding through the room, I sought a congenial face, perhaps one leading to the "movie-like adventure" Leonardo had promised but saw none.

"Congratulations," a voice boomed as a hand touched my shoulder.

I turned and looked upward into the smile of a tall, familiar-looking man in his sixties.

"I do know you," I said quizzically, being unable to remember his name.

"But I remember you. Leonardo introduced us as you were leaving a restaurant two months ago."

"Then you were in uniform, Commissioner," I said, with a burst of remembrance.

He smiled again and led me toward a sofa.

"Can I get you a drink?" he asked.

"Just water, I don't drink," I said, trying not to sound prim.

"A good habit, unlike alcohol which is a habit best left unacquired. I'll join you."

As he left, I remembered what Leonardo said about talking to a stranger. That one should try to discover their ambition, who they are and what they really want. But what could the Commissioner want of a young unemployed lawyer descended from an executed murderer. Suppressing this thought, I smilingly glanced about the room, hoping to present the image of an older debutante.

Upon his return, we silently sipped lemon-sliced ice water, taking each other's measure.

"I have a daughter your age, also a lawyer. And call me Jim," he said.

"What law school did she attend, Jim?" I asked.

"Yale, she wanted a smaller class than Columbia," he said.

"Where is she working now?" I asked.

"She's not. She's trying to figure out where she belongs, what she wants in life."

"That's not easy," I said.

"It's not," he said, with a firmness that indicated he had something else on his mind.

Chapter 72

"Have you considered your future?" the Commissioner asked.

"That's complicated," I parried.

"It's a complicated time," I said.

I smiled, sensing that he was formulating a suggestion.

"I like smart people and your academic achievements were considerable. A law degree permits several career paths. Working at a law firm with its overwork and drudgery. Working as a public defender with the same drawbacks and more internal politicizing, or something else. The Central Intelligence Agency hires lawyers too."

"Please. Can you see me as a spy?" I said with a laugh.

"No," he said with a laugh. "Your beauty makes you too noticeable but maybe if you put on a hundred pounds."

I just smiled. He was taking his time.

"Okay, enough of the introduction. I want you to work for me," he said firmly.

Now my response wasn't amusement but an open-mouthed stare.

"You must be joking," I said.

"Why?

"Because. Do you know who I am," I said firmly.

"I know you're very smart."

"And?"

"More about your father than you likely know. Do you know that he was once an America hero with commendations to prove it?"

I sat open-mouthed until I began crying.

"I'm sorry. I didn't mean to upset you," he said.

"How could I not be upset? You're talking about the only parent that loved me whatever his crimes."

"And why you battled to attend his execution," Jim said.

Dead To Life

"To the end I vowed, his and mine," I said.
He silently waited as I dried my eyes,
"Accepting my job offer would burnish his memory," he
said.

Chapter 73

"I want you to help me. You would work directly with me, in an office down the hall from mine at One Police Plaza. No one else will know your identity. You can choose whatever name you like."

My weak smile caused his "What?"

"While a media sensation I wore different disguises. I wouldn't want to return to that," I said.

"And you won't. Adopting a pseudonym would be useful for the work but not to hide you. If things work out I'll present you with the NYPD Commendation for Community Service. In a public ceremony with bagpipes and all," he said.

"Bagpipes would make it seem more a funeral. But okay, exactly what would I be doing?" I said.

"It's critical to maintain the public's trust in police. The IAB, Internal Affairs Bureau, investigates allegations of corruption and misconduct and I've heard rumors that some of our civilian, sensitively placed workers, have what might be called *two bosses*.

"Rumors of doing what?" I asked.

"You'll learn that when you agree. What do you think?"

"As a new city worker I don't imagine I'd be paid much," I said, to give me time to think.

"It's a voluntary position but you don't need the money," he said.

"You've done your checking," I said.

"Always."

I continued parrying, thinking of my intention to work with Leonardo

"It's an interesting proposal. How many hours would you expect me to work?"

"Being a volunteer that's entirely up to you. You'd be free to come and go as you wish. No one will watch your hours or, apart from me, know what you're doing. We'll pick a boring title for your role."

"How about President of the Young Ladies Police Benefit Fundraising Society?" I said, with a smile.

"That sounds innocuous enough."

"And boring too."

"Bored is one thing you won't be. That I'll guarantee!" he said and offered his hand.

Chapter 74

I hesitated but not for long. Gripping his hand in agreement as does a drowning person hoping for a lifeline. I looked *good*, even possibly beautiful as the Commissioner described me, but was fragile. Lacking self-confidence and sturdy sense of who I was, what psychologists term an *identity*, I was only too happy to latch myself to a strong person who would provide me with a purpose in life. Which parents usually foster in their developing teenager and I had lacked.

"When will I learn more?" I asked, with interest.

"Soon, within several days to a week. I'll send you a secure phone. Use it only to contact me. Do you sleep alone?"

"No, it's not that," he said with a laugh upon seeing my expression. "Though it might be if I were thirty years younger. I don't want you questioned if I phone after midnight."

"That would be fine. I'm very much alone," I said.

"It's probably how you survived," he said.

Hearing those words I felt understood like when I spoke with Leonardo. How odd they were socially connected too, I thought.

"I'd best mingle. We'll soon speak on the phone, rarely meeting in the future," he said.

"Yes, Jim," I said, accepting my marching orders and receiving his warm parting smile.

Ingrid drew by my side.

"I noticed you speaking with the Commissioner for a long time," she said.

"He's an interesting man," I said cryptically.

"Too old for you," she said, with a smile.

"Well, there are other things in life too, you know," I said, and winked.

Chapter 75

While others partied, I continued playing my role of grateful graduate, though one of little value since I had not yet passed the bar exam. Dropping witty rejoinders like, "the only nice thing about rich men is when they lose their money," accompanied with small flirtatious touches, I was the belle of the evening, and by far the youngest.

Did these powerful men view me as potential protege or mistress, I asked myself, my mind having become freed from restraint by the courteously offered cocktails I indulged. Ingrid sidled beside me during a rare moment when I stood alone.

"Be careful," Ingrid warned.

"Always," I said in drunken slur.

"I mean it, you're drunk. Are you sleeping here tonight?"

"Leonardo suggested it. He said travel isn't safe in early morning even in this neighborhood," I said.

"The advice of a caring father," Ingrid said.

"I have my pistol," I said somewhat incoherently.

"That's it. You're staying here tonight!" Ingrid said,

I didn't object when she gripped my arm, knowing good advice when I hear it.

We fled upstairs as the first guest departed, sped by Leonardo's quip of it being "the youngsters' bedtime." Whether reflecting concern or criticism I was too dazed to care.

After being awakened by an unremembered dream after a fitful three-hour sleep, I studied my surroundings. The room was both comfortable and luxurious, casual but formal with oak wood flooring, exposed wood beams, glass chandelier, and tall narrow windows to maximize sunlight. A room whose beauty seemed to mock my despair, and throbbing question.

"What was the question?" Doctor Hess had asked.

"It was about Jim, the Police Commissioner, but Leonardo too," I said.

117

Chapter 76

"I couldn't help wondering about their similarities, why I so easily latched onto both so quickly," I said.

"How do you feel they were similar?" Doctor Hess had asked.

"Certainly physically, both being tall with broad chests, gravelly voice, and muscly fingers. But they also had the gift of inspiration, the ability to project the gravitational pull of your best future like my father did with me," I said.

"And it appears that he had once been a good man in his life, even a hero," Doctor Hess said.

"He was always my hero," I said crossly.

"When did the Commissioner describe his heroic deed, what earned him his medal?"

"Not until later, as if it were a reward that I need earn," I said.

Despite the lingering effect of alcohol I managed to fall back to sleep. Awakening a little before ten, to send a reassuring text to my grandmother and another to Roman asking that he pick me up at two. Ingrid knocked and entered a few minutes later, with a big grin and bearing a tray of food. She was becoming the best female friend I never had.

"Hungry?" she asked.

"I never have much of an appetite except for chocolate which I try to avoid. This morning I feel less likely to eat than usual," I said.

"It's the alcohol but try. You'll need energy for what I've planned for us today," she said.

"I asked to be picked up at two. Will it last later?"

"Definitely! Maybe until tonight or even tomorrow," she said with an infectious grin.

"What is it?" I insisted with aroused curiosity.

Dead To Life

"We'll be meeting my newly discovered brother," she said triumphantly.

Chapter 77

Ingrid's revelation floored me.

"You're brave," I said.

"Not really. Just hoping that somewhere out there is a better family for me than I lucked into," she said.

"How did you find him?" I asked.

"Easier than finding the Bazooka Cherry Berry Bubble Gum I keep handy," Ingrid said.

"Okay, but how did you do it?" I asked, feeling floored by her words.

"It was like ordering on eBay and only cost one-hundred-nineteen dollars. Additions added information about health risks but I wasn't interested, just the Ancestry Service. It's done at home without blood or needles. They send you a kit, you spit in the tube they provide and register using its barcode, then mail it back in the prepaid package. So simple even a lawyer could do it."

"Considering my family, I'd be afraid to learn my relatives," I said, wrinkling my nose.

"Oh come on! I'm sure they'd be the same species," Ingrid deadpanned.

"Right! You're in a jovial mood," I said.

"Hiding terror and why you're coming with me," she said, in a pleading tone.

"Sure, and with my pistol," I said reassuringly."

"I hope it doesn't come to that," Ingrid said, without a smile.

"Surely not. Then the company would have to send your heir a refund," I said.

Ingrid didn't make a rejoinder, and I apologized.

"I'm sorry. I'm nervous and my jokes seem an acquired taste that most never got," I said.

Ingrid just nodded, touched my hand, and I dressed. Then me and my first Best Female Friend went to meet her new brother.

Chapter 78

"We'll walk, to clear your mind," Ingrid said as we left Leonardo's mansion.

Her comment didn't faze me, feeling that I was basking in our friendship.

Foreigners, which is how New York City residents consider others, don't realize how territorial the five boroughs are with Manhattan being exceptionally so. The world famed Fifth Avenue divides into the East and West Side with different vibes though the same obscenely high rents.

Her brother's East Side apartment was a half-mile south of Leonardo's home. We walked quickly alongside stylishly dressed passersby, mothers pushing strollers, and the homeless who gained brief guilt-ridden stares.

The doorman of his apartment building announced us with a smile, and only then did I remember that Ingrid hadn't told me her brother's name.

"It's Gunter," she said.

"'Thomas' one can familiarly call 'Tom' but what can one call 'Gunter?'" I asked.

"Beats me. We'll let him tell us," Ingrid said.

But this information was to come later since the person opening his door wasn't Gunter but a suited cold-faced fifties woman who barricaded the entrance.

"Good afternoon," she said, without a hint of warmth,

"I'm here to see Gunter. I brought my friend too," Ingrid stammered.

"I know who you are. Gunter's alleged sister. I'm Edith Correll, an attorney hired by his mother to protect his interests," she said.

Hmm, I thought, you didn't have to be a lawyer to know this meeting wasn't off to a promising start.

Chapter 79

The wealthy have a way of being removed from the real world and the wealth of Gunter's family was obvious. The size of their apartment and many uniformed building employees told me that.

Moreover, the rich *expect* dishonesty from strangers, expecting them to try to separate them from their money which gives them status and more. This I understood, betrayal having been a way of life in my family. Thus, feeling at home so to speak and because our reception had struck Ingrid dumb, I took the lead.

"I'm Ingrid's friend and also an attorney though we didn't consider our meeting with Gunter as having legal ramifications. Ingrid wants only to meet him and has no interest in his finances. Will they be permitted to speak?"

Though being on the tip of my tongue I didn't add that Gunter is an adult. For all we knew his mother might still bathe him.

"Let them in," came a commanding voice.

The door opened fully and we stepped inside.

From within the spacious foyer I saw that the apartment took up two floors.

Gunter's mother wasn't the battle axe I expected. Instead, she was tall, slim, and wore a coral floral, pleated midi dress with voluminous sleeves and tiered skirt lifted by a layer of crinoline. Like something out of a 1950s dance hall it indicated both individuality and wealth. I judged its cost at about seven-hundred-dollars.

"I apologize for your reception but we're a cautious family. Can I offer you coffee, tea or, it being afternoon, perhaps sherry?"

I looked toward Ingrid. This decision was hers.

Chapter 80

Ingrid requested tea, as I would have chosen, this perhaps indicating we were on the same wavelength. It also suggested modesty and decorum, unlike the association of coffee with business and wine with friendship and intimacy.

A maid scurried off with this order and we sat on opposing sofas. Glancing toward the door, I wondered when Gunter would join us but my hint wasn't taken. Tea arrived and Ingrid's audition began.

Lawyer Correll stared.

"Tell us about yourself," she demanded coldly.

"I'm ordinary with no secret agenda," Ingrid stammered.

"She has no secret agenda. Ingrid wants only to meet her brother," I reiterated.

"Tell us your background, schooling and the like," Martha asked her.

We earlier learned her name when Ingrid studied Gunter online.

"As I said, it's ordinary. I grew up and learned to speak English at school in Stockholm. Worked as an airline stewardess before studying finance at the London School of Economics. I live in Manhattan and work at a hedge fund where I earn a substantial income. I have no interest in your family's money and the idea that I seek an affair with my newly discovered brother is preposterous. I would hope you would want to know me too," Ingrid replied, anger seeping into her words.

Which seemed the right tone to take since it lowered the temperature of the discussion.

"I apologize," Martha said.. "I'm alone and can be *too* cautious about Gunter. He's my only child, one that I never thought I would have after two miscarriages and interminable sessions of In Vitro Fertilization. My husband died last year after our long struggle with his pancreatic cancer."

"I'm very sorry. No one can is ever ready for the death of a loved one," Ingrid said, with feeling.

At that something surprising happened. Martha sprang toward Ingrid and hugged her.

Chapter 81

"Gunter was looking forward to meeting you but he sprained an ankle playing volleyball this morning. It swelled so he's at our doctor's office. He should be home shortly," Martha said.

"I've had that. It hurts," Ingrid said.

Whether the feeling she expressed was authentic or feigned I couldn't say but Martha seemed appreciative.

"We've had too much sorrow in our family," she said, and her gaze turned toward me.

"Have we met before?" she asked.

I spoke quickly, being continually mindful of my past media celebrity.

"I don't think so though maybe while shopping at Saks or Tiffany," I said with a measure of class consciousness.

"Perhaps," she said.

Her stare made me uneasy, just as Gunter arrived to save our bacon so to speak. Though unashamed of my past, speaking of it would have added unwelcome distraction to the meeting.

Gunter's appearance helped me understand his mother's concern. Being wealthy and twenty-eight, Tall, single, and handsome with striking blue eyes, he would be considered dreamy by virtually every unattached woman who attracted his glance. And, though this wasn't my social meeting, I felt lust for him too. His manners were perfect and his limp made him even more desirable. Just the man needing my care, a woman would tell herself.

"I'm terribly sorry. It's rude to be late," he said.

His enticing sheepish smile must add to Ingrid's regret they're related, I thought. It also aroused my desire to hug him, which bothered me.

"Why do you think it bothered you?" Doctor Hess had asked.

Answering this took thinking and it was some time before I responded.

"My father made it clear that I was to trust no one except immediate family. This instilled a caution that dominated my dealings with anyone other than them, and influenced the self-reliance I developed," I said.

"It also explains why you had no close friends growing up," Doctor Hess said.

I simply nodded agreement.

Chapter 82

I watched Gunter and Ingrid chat, being the unneeded guest with a fascinated couple. Martha left but shortly returned with a print-out she handed me. I knew what it was without looking.

"I thought you were her," she said without emotion.

"It's me," I admitted, looking directly into her face.

"You were so brave, at such a young age too. How could you bear watching your father's execution?" she asked.

I always refused to answer this question from reporters but did so now. Why I wasn't sure but maybe the joyful sight of Ingrid and Gunter together had aroused my thought of the family I lacked.

"I had to go. He was my father and I loved him," I said, and began crying.

"Is there anything I can do?" Martha asked, seating herself beside me.

"No, but thanks. Having a responsive person to share it with is enough. I rarely cried about it before. Maybe I needed to be older and more settled in life to risk it.

"What are your plans?" Martha asked.

"I had none for years, being forced by publicity into home tutoring and wearing disguises when outside. I decided to study law after realizing its power, that it gained what everyone considered impossible: forcing the government to permit a fourteen-year-old to watch her father's execution. I just graduated law school. My father would have been proud," I said between sobs.

"He was a complex man," Martha said, charitably.

"And was once a military hero," I said proudly.

Chapter 83

Martha started, as did I when I'd learned this. Which I shouldn't have revealed since it came from the Police Commissioner after stressing the secrecy of our relationship. Not much of a secret agent am I? I asked myself ruefully.

Her question came quickly and wasn't surprising.

"What did he do?" she asked.

Now what do I say? I thought.

"What did you reply?" Doctor Hess had asked.

"It wasn't that hard. Being deceitful was the watchword in my family," I said with a smile. "I said it came from what my father told me when I was very young. He'd been away and I was angry and wouldn't talk to him, like little kids can be. Until he said that he'd been helping the government far away in Europe. Doing important business for which Americans would be grateful if they knew. But that what he'd done was a secret that he couldn't tell even me and that I must never tell anyone. We made a pinky promise I would keep the secret, which I did until blurting it out now."

"How did Martha respond?" Doctor Hess asked.

"Again, as I expected. That had this been known it might have prevented his execution," she said.

"He wouldn't permit it. I asked him this during our last meeting the night before. He said he'd done bad things which no earlier goodness could remedy, and that though those he murdered were evil couldn't atone for it. Moreover, the government would deny knowledge of his activity since the diplomatic repercussions would be great were his deeds made public. 'It's best I carry them to the grave,'" he said.

Martha listened silently and when she spoke her words seemed to inaugurate a special bond between us.

"I understand why your father is your hero. I would have loved him too," she said.

Chapter 84

Without conscious intention, I kept spilling secrets of personal memories, though not anything to which the Commissioner would have objected. Feeling myself in a trance-like state, driven by a hidden force that defied rational behavior.

Forcing myself to breathe slowly, I sank into the deep cushions. Though many years had passed, its memory was still painful. Reminding me of what was quickly lost but fearing to speak until the pain lifted.

"Do you know the musical drama, *The Threepenny Opera*, written by Bertolt Brecht in 1928?" I asked.

"No," Martha answered.

"It was my father's favorite. Adapted from John Gay's 1728 play, *The Beggars Opera*, which tells of an antihero gangster, Macheath who marries Polly Peachum, the daughter of a ring of London beggars. Her father contrives to have Macheath arrested but he escapes until being betrayed by a prostitute to the police. Though condemned to the gallows, he is saved by a last-minute pardon on Queen Victoria's coronation day. During our last moments together, my father spoke several of the opera's lines:

'Some are out there in the darkness,
Others out there in the light,
If they're in the light we see them,
In the dark they're out of sight.'"

"It must have been a powerful moment," Martha said.

"It was and I finally felt at peace when I just cried, as he is now," I said.

Chapter 85

Martha became another of my few allies in life, even closer after what she revealed. Creating a unique experience for one who had cherished her isolation despite the Biblical injunction praising closeness?

"Now much did you learn of our family tree from the gene analysis?" Martha asked.

"From what Ingrid told me, only of your son," I said.

"It didn't extend to past generations?" she asked.

"Not unless they signed up with 23andMe," I said, wondering what she was getting at.

"You've never heard of Fritz Kolbe?" she asked.

"No," I said.

"Let me tell you a story," she said, and did.

"Fritz Kolbe was the only American spy in Germany during World War Two and President Roosevelt himself read the secrets he sent. Authentic reports transmitted by German diplomatic, military, and intelligence sources to their headquarters. He had the code name, "George Wood," and his reports were classified under the title 'Boston series.'"

"Other German resisters of the Nazi regime were honored after the war but not him. He died of gallbladder cancer in 1969 and only a dozen people attended his funeral. Two unknown men laid a wreath on behalf of Richard Helms, Director of the CIA. Before his death, Allen Dulles wrote of Kolbe's integrity, the great role he played in Hitler's overthrow, and the tragedy it wasn't recognized in his own country. Kolbe was my father and his genes are part of us," she said.

"He was an unknown hero," I said.

"Like your father. Can you guess the greatest of my life's regrets?" she asked fervently.

Believing that her question was rhetorical I didn't answer, as it was.

Dead To Life

"That I never had a daughter like you," she said, gripping my hand.

Chapter 86

The afternoon drifted by as if in a trance. Martha showed me the rest of her spacious apartment, indicating a bedroom where I might sleep after spending a night in town. I thanked her, both knowing that we'd passed a point in our undefinable relationship. My not being a daughter but far more than a mere acquaintance. Maybe a trusted confidante but we would see.

Just as all good things come to an end, so did the bonding of Gunter and Ingrid. They hugged before we left as Martha and I shared understanding smiles.

"How did it go?" I asked Ingrid as we left the building.

"Swimmingly. We're going clubbing tomorrow night. Come with us!"

"I'd be a third wheel. Maybe after the two of you have spoken more," I said.

"It isn't like that," Ingrid said, though not pressing her invitation.

We returned to Leonardo's mansion in a comfortable silence. The maid was still cleaning-up from my graduation party so we went to her bedroom which resembled more motel style than artful décor.

"It's just another of the guest bedrooms. I don't spend much time here," she said.

No explanation was needed and I said nothing.

"Why do you still live at home? Is it financial?" she asked.

"No, not at all. Because it's comfortable and where I feel safe. My father's death traumatized me, and my grandmother needs me too," I said.

"I understand. I'm not sure I survive what you did," Ingrid said.

"Your life was just as bad," I said.

"Maybe, but if you ever need a place to hang out..." Ingrid said.

"Thank you. I will," I said, smiling broadly.

You've gained good friends today, I told myself, with a feeling of achievement.

Chapter 87

It had been a long day emotionally and Ingrid needed to talk. Lying in bed, she described her afternoon with Gunter as I reclined on the opposing chaise lounge.

"If we weren't related I would fall for him," she said.

"It seems you already have," I said.

"I did, but..."

"It's the *buts* that get you in life," I said.

"Our talk quickly got intimate so maybe we both hungered for the connection. I asked why so eligible a man as he wasn't married and he told me."

Her silence continued until I finally asked, "Why?"

"He does have a girlfriend, Hannah, a friend he's known since kindergarten when she took it upon herself to look after him. If the others played a game and he wasn't included she'd insist he was."

"So what happened?" I asked.

"The worst ever."

This time I waited and, when Ingrid spoke, it wasn't something I wanted to hear.

"Four months ago, Hannah and her mother were visiting a friend in Queens. During a home invasion, the two older women were murdered and Hannah was raped and left for dead. She's still recovering," Ingrid said.

Though no comforting words were truly possible of such horror, I tried.

"*Hannah* means *grace*. Until his death my father had been my whole world. After his death I turned to the Bible and tried to make sense of what happened. The word *grace* occurs many times in the Old and New Testaments. It is the concept of God as being the watchful master of one who receives mercy and favor," I said.

We didn't speak again until dinner.

135

Chapter 88

We ate dinner alone. Leonardo was out at a "business meeting," which might have involved another girl-friend but I didn't say.

Conversation labored, too much having recently happened for both of us. My view of my father had undergone a cataclysmic shift. Not that I could have loved him more since he'd been an admirable father no matter his murderous deeds. But never in my wildest fantasy had I imagined him a hero. Maybe someday the Police Commissioner will relate his deeds. And hearing of Hannah's experience had greatly affected me too.

"Why do you think that was?" Doctor Hess had asked me.

"I'm not sure. A boy once touched me on the street. I told you that. Or maybe because I always felt on edge, as if a Satanic creature pursued me."

"You said the Biblical name, Hannah, means one who receives mercy. Having been deserted by your mother, perhaps it's what you yearn for and why the name affected you strongly," he said.

Risking our friendship, I had asked Ingrid what might have been too personal a question.

"How long will you stay with Leonardo?"

Ingrid smiled instead of exhibiting the scowl that I feared,

"I haven't yet decided that very good question," she said deliberately.

I waited, expecting her to elaborate and she did, being more revealing than I expected.

"I don't want Leonardo as an enemy so our breakup must be mutual. Him tiring of me or acquiring another lover, as I suspect he has. But I'd have to get a job, and apartments here are outrageously expensive."

"With your economics degree and languages, getting a job shouldn't be hard," I said.

Ingrid smiled.

"What about the apartment?" she asked.

"I'll rent one and you could stay with me," I said, surprising even myself.

Chapter 89

Though the thought of renting an apartment had surprised me, it came as a shock to my grandmother despite her attempt to conceal it.

"Being twenty-four, I suppose it's time but will you be safe living alone?" she asked.

"I won't be alone. I'll have a roommate who works in the city," I said.

Though seemingly acquiescent, my grandmother's face darkened and Roman took up the fray.

"Considering your wealth and family's past, you'll always be a target and I don't like it," he said firmly.

Being far more family member than employee, I took his objection seriously.

"You're right but I can't live here forever. What would you advise?" I asked reasonably.

The speed of his answer aroused my thought that it had been long prepared.

"You'll need a bodyguard I trust," he said.

The size of my apartment suddenly changed from two to three-bedrooms.

"Okay. Can you find me one?" I agreed.

"I have just the lady in mind," he said, smiling

My grandmother smiled too.

"We'll invite her for lunch tomorrow," she said.

Their smiles caused me to wonder how long they'd planned this.

I met my future bodyguard, April, the next day. Being tall, slim, and in her late twenties, she would grace a club scene and could do more.

"She's a competitive shooter and Krav Maga trainer. She'll tell you about that," Roman said, and she did.

"Krav Maga means *contact combat*. It's a martial art developed for the Israel Defense Forces and derives from aikido, judo, karate and boxing techniques. It focuses on real-world situations and efficiency.

"Emphasizing simultaneous defensive and aggressive moves, its basic principle is to avoid physical confrontation. But if this is impossible, to end the fight quickly with attacks at the most vulnerable parts of the body regardless if they cause injury or death. Striking the opponent until they're incapacitated, with any object at hand, at the body's most vulnerable points such as eyes, throat, or groin. All while staying aware of surroundings to deal with other threats and seeking escape routes."

Impressed, I asked, "What was your last job?"

"I worked for a government agency abroad. My supervisor became *familiar* one night and I forcefully objected. It was suggested that my talents lay elsewhere."

My dad would be proud of her, I thought, and smiled.

Chapter 90

My thought of moving came quicker than the actual move. A common bitching session of law school students had concerned housing: where in Manhattan to live, the other boroughs being termed *Siberia,* and how to find an apartment with a not-too shocking rent. One with a *reasonable* rent didn't exist except for the fortunate few who'd inherited a rent-controlled apartment.

Thanks to my inheritance, I wasn't paralyzed by such concern. Comfort and safety were primary and I left the latter judgment to Roman. "Security is my profession," he would scold when I slipped up.

April, Ingrid, and I quickly became a threesome. Though I'd pay the rent I considered it crucial that the apartment was one we all liked if not loved.

"He's a better show than I've seen on Broadway," Ingrid whispered as the realtor took us to view our first apartment.

A tall, handsome, well-dressed man in his thirties, Mr. Galbreath ("call me Ted") was recommended to Ingrid by a stranger who chatted her up in a Starbucks that week. Despite this dubious warrant, Ted was a consummate professional, being described in a local weekly publication as having "incredible magnetism." Leader of one of the most successful real estate sales teams in the nation, he was also said to have "a killer instinct." This gave me pause but only for a moment.

"It's sales jargon," Ingrid explained.

I got it.

Chapter 91

Renting a Manhattan apartment introduced me to a novel experience. Attending agent-sponsored sales openings at party-catered, decorated apartments mobbed with desperate renters and hungry models.

"What agency are you with?" a man asked.

His compliment boosted my morale but his intent was more my body than my goal. I gave him a vague smile and wandered to another room.

There, a man wearing the realtor badge approached. "Your parents are exceptional, willing to pay this high rent," he said, in a tone that managed to be both complimentary and deprecating.

"No, I'm paying. What's the cost fully furnished?" I asked.

Hoping to conceal his embarrassment by riffling through the papers he held, he said. "Nine-thousand a month unfurnished, furnished is a thousand more."

"How long is the lease?" I asked.

"That's negotiable."

"Everything is negotiable. I'm a lawyer. What's your best offer?" I asked evenly.

"Okay. A three-year lease gets a fifteen-percent discount and a two-year lease gets a ten-percent discount."

"What 's my discount for payment in advance?" I asked.

"Well, perhaps we could arrange one-percent discount," he said, with evident surprise.

"Is that the best you can do?"

"Two-percent and you won't be charged extra for use of the building's recreation center," he said.

I pretended to be thinking, having learned in law school that not immediately agreeing to an offer is the best negotiating tactic. I let the silence build between us.

Dead To Life

"Give me your card. I'll see what my roommates think about the apartment," I said finally.

Chapter 92

Finding my prospective roommates took a few minutes in this spacious apartment. Nor was speaking with them a snap since their plan for that evening differed from mine. Hooking-up was their game and they were well into it with Ingrid sitting on a man's lap and April's hand being held by another.

Since April was an employee, I chose to interrupt her first. Hesitantly, since interfering with a woman's love quest is the fastest way to end their relationship.

"Can I drag April away for just a minute to get her opinion about the apartment?" I asked the man while touching his arm.

Having such downcast tone and pleading eyes that I had the passing thought I should have studied acting and not law.

He smilingly agreed and I tugged April to a vacant sofa out of earshot.

"Would you be happy in this apartment?" I asked.

"Absolutely, but the rent must be stiff," she said enthusiastically.

"Let me worry about that. I'm taking it furnished so check the bedrooms for first claim," I said.

"It's certainly grander than the shared motel rooms the government shoehorned me into," she said.

"I want you to be happy. I might need your protection for a long time," I said.

"You're in that great danger?" she asked, in a sudden change of mood.

"Did you see the old movie, *Chinatown*? I asked, after a thoughtful silence.

"No."

"The plot is of an ethical policeman who became a private detective. A woman hires him to check if her husband is having an affair. He tries to dissuade her, saying it's best to let sleeping dogs lay, but she refuses his advice. He investigates, sees her husband going rowing with a teenage girl, and tells the wife. The man is the local Water Department's Commissioner, the detective's finding is leaked, and a scandal erupts that threatens the husband's job."

"Why are you telling me this?" April interrupted, eager to return to her prospective beau.

"You'll understand in a minute," I said.

"When the scandal breaks, another woman comes to the detective's office and asks if the detective has ever seen her. He says 'no' and she says *she* is the Water Commissioner's wife and storms from his office, her parting words being that he'll hear from her lawyer.

"To cut to the chase: the Commissioner is murdered by his wife's father, a wealthy power-broker who wanted a lucrative but potentially dangerous dam built, the girl that the Commissioner rowed with is both his wife's sister and her child, resulting from incest with her father.

"To safeguard her daughter from her monstrous father she shoots but only wounds him, then flees with her daughter but is accidently shot and killed by the police after which her screaming daughter is grabbed by father/grandfather. This happened in the city's Chinatown, with all having resulted from the detective's laudable effort to discover the truth. I have an odd feeling that my life is entering Chinatown," I said.

My smile before leaving to find Ingrid wasn't reassuring.

Chapter 93

"What are you thinking about?" Doctor Hess had asked after a period of silence.

"My talk with April, at the apartment's rental party," I said.

"What happened?" he asked after another long silence.

"I spoke first with Ingrid. She liked the apartment too and I said she could have first digs on bedroom and I would take last."

"That was kind," Doctor Hess said.

"Where I sleep never bothered me," I sniffed.

This silence was broken by my sobbing and then words.

"After leaving the party my thinking turned from it to me. My never having learned what women pick up as teenagers. How to be seductive with a man, as April and Ingrid knew instinctively, expressing interest by batting eyes and touching.

"Ingrid once told me that as a child she played a counting and divination game to foretell her romantic future: 'Tinker, tailor, soldier, sailor...What will my husband be?' Why hadn't I?" I pleadingly asked.

"Maybe because surviving in your family meant not relying on anyone. Though loving your father and he loving you, you lacked a mother to teach you feminine ways. The romances that you read and movies you watched entice you but were placed in a compartment of your mind separate from others. To protect you from the danger of intimacy but also condemned you to solitude. It's a powerful unconscious battle," Doctor Hess said.

"Can I change?" I asked hopefully.

"Yes, but it won't be easy or painless," he said sympathetically.

Now the silence was longer, the session was over, and I rose to leave.

"I feel close to you now. Maybe it's the first step," I said.

Chapter 94

My move was both tearful and joyous. Unhappy because it meant leaving the only home I'd known and the two remaining people who loved me: my grandmother and Roman. Yet joyous too since renting the apartment accomplished my final hurdle into adulthood after completing schooling and thanks to my inheritance.

My grandmother hugged me and Roman vowed eternal vigilance over my safety. He drove me to the apartment, leaving the porter to carry my luggage inside, and it was over.

Ingrid and April had established themselves earlier and arranged a celebratory luncheon. Knowing my preference for healthy food it was, shall I say, *interesting*. Organic Chili containing brown rice, chickpeas, kidney beans, textured soy protein and more. Miso Soup consisting of miso broth, peas, and vegetables. Potatoes with mushroom gravy and sauerkraut. For dessert there were brownies and peanut butter cookies, washed down with a choice of black tea, green tea, or Carrot Detox for those feeling the need.

Conversation sparkled as they shared their life troubles. Ingrid told of the sexual abuse by her brother to which April bluntly remarked, "I would have killed the bastard but why didn't you run away?"

"It wouldn't have been easy. Since my only way out seemed another relationship, I told a schoolmate I loved him and we should run away but he thought me crazy. What really imprisoned me was feeling psychologically trapped."

A belief which I easily related to, as I did with April's embarrassment when she told her tale of woe.

Chapter 95

April's experience wasn't the shame of having a killer-for-hire father but almost as bad.

"Government agencies are stingy so they have workers share bedrooms and not in a Hilton either. We'd been trailing a trainee intelligence agent in Washington, his assignment being to meet an alleged foreign spy without being observed. Unfortunately for his grade, we easily filmed their meeting before returning to the motel to relax.

"My much older married roommate had many friends in the department's upper management. The room had twin beds and I awoke in the middle of the night to find him atop me. My saying 'Don't. You don't want to do this' had no affect so I acted instinctively. The scratches on his face were the least painful of what I did but I can't imagine how he explained them to his wife.

"That incident ended my future with the agency. They were afraid to fire me but got me transferred to a job filing historic classified documents in the basement. I took the hint, went private, and here I am."

"And I'm glad you are. To us, the Three Musketeers!" I exclaimed, raising my cup of tea.

But there were no smiles as we toasted.

Chapter 96

The apartment furnishings were decorator created, artistic but not homelike.

"Crafting a home takes time," Ingrid responded to my complaint.

So, as women do when at loose ends, we went shopping. Not for beds and sofas since large items were present but for the small things which make a house a home as they say. Buying a comfortable rustic gray, oak wood adjustable office chair, white steel bookends, a grey textured Terracotta table vase, and a beige rug. Would a decorator have chosen these? Probably not but they were for *our* home, and the shopping freed me from thinking what came next.

April's immediate future was already decided since, as my bodyguard, she would trail after me. But what was I going to do?

Law school was over and I felt confident about passing the state licensing exam. Long an obsessive student, exams had never been a problem but what to do next was. To seek a job with Leonardo or another firm or concentrate on how the Police Commissioner would use me? *Use me?* I thought sourly. Would I always be *used*?

My answer came that evening. A text from the Commissioner asking that we meet next morning in Chinatown.

Chapter 97

The restaurant was a hole-in-the-wall on Mott Street, noticeable only for the auto parked outside. A black town car guarded by the tall, stern-faced man leaning on it. Who ignored us after giving a hard stare as we entered the shop. It was empty of customers except for the Commissioner.

"Who is she?" he asked, nodding toward April.

"I'm her bodyguard, former Agency. I saw yours outside," she said.

"Do you feel you need a bodyguard with me?" he asked rhetorically.

"As much as you need one with me," I answered cheekily.

"Touche. Hungry?" he asked with a smile.

I wasn't but accepted the proffered menu. Eating gives time to think and size up the coming offer, I was taught in law school.

"The food here is authentic. I'm starting with Xiao long bao but you probably shouldn't," he said, in response to our puzzled looks.

"It's a steamed dumpling which the Shanghai government declared a national treasure in 2006, a bit like America's undeclared apple pie. It's pork-based cubes steamed inside a bun that bursts into warm soup when poked into. It's to be slurped quickly, hot off the steaming basket, but takes care to be eaten without spilling on yourself or burning your mouth with the hot liquid. You must transfer the bun to a spoon and take a small bite off the top of the dumpling. Then let the steam from the soup inside cool before slurping it down and popping the rest of the dumpling in your mouth," he said.

Being a semi-vegetarian, his mention of pork and lengthy caution made me feel nearly ill.

"I'll pass," I said, scanning the menu.

Chapter 98

Being of Italian/Swedish descent, Chow Mein was the extent of my knowledge about Chinese cuisine. Thankfully, beside each item on the menu was its description and colorful history.

I scanned it for meatless items, choosing Jianbing, a crepe layered with beaten egg, cilantro, and green onions covered in hoisin sauce. Then Tang yuan, a sweet dish of rice balls, symbolic of harmony and reunion and eaten by Chinese families at their New Year according to the menu.

Though being endangered here was inconceivable, I felt reassured that Ingrid ordered only tea. Her task was my protection, not social. The Commissioner waited until the waiter left before speaking further.

"Thank you for coming at such an early hour," he said.

"I expected the matter was important," I said, meeting his courtesy half-way.

"It is. How much do you know about computer security?" he asked.

"Only what I picked up from reading online articles," I said.

"OK. Not everyone is well informed or follows what they should do. We're confronting a situation that you may be able to help us with. Now it's the life of one kidnapped child but soon maybe more."

The waiter reappeared, served, and instantly left following the Commissioner's hand gesture.

"I'm a novice lawyer and know nothing of such matters. Why do you feel I can help?" I asked, feeling uneasy.

"I wouldn't ask unless I thought you could. You see, you're friends with the person who we believe is close to the kidnapper," he said.

I felt momentarily dizzy as thoughts of my father's criminal life arose. Which must have shown since the Commissioner spoke quickly.

"No! I know you have nothing to do with the kidnapping or even that you know this person well. But you can get closer to him than anyone we have, and with the appearance of innocence too. Will you help us?" he asked.

"How could I refuse?" I replied instantly.

"I was sure you'd say that." the Commissioner said warmly, smiling and reaching for my hand.

Chapter 99

As the Commissioner spoke, I felt my life moving onto a new path. My intent to establish a legal career vanished, replaced by...what? Law enforcement? Though I could never escape my identity as the child of a hitman. Or maybe simply that of a concerned citizen. My eyes glanced over the proverbs printed on the placemat: "When adversity comes, receive it favorably." and "The timber is already a boat; the rice is cooked."

"You seem far away. What are you thinking?" the Commissioner asked.

"These proverbs took my mind," I said.

The Commissioner motioned to the waiter who had been watching us from the counter. When he neared, the Commissioner asked, "Please help us, Hong. What do these proverbs mean?"

Hong nodded, smiled, and studied the lines. "With pleasure, sir. The first advises to take things as they come; the second that what is done cannot be undone."

"Wisdom of the Ages," the Commissioner said, and Hong bowed reverently before leaving.

"I'm more than committed. Endangered children pull at me emotionally, so much that I can't finish a movie or novel containing it," I said.

"Maybe you felt endangered as a child," the Commissioner said sympathetically.

"I had a painful childhood," I said simply, surprised by his insight.

"Let's get this child back," he said firmly.

Chapter 100

"Who's the child?" I asked.

"The six-year-old daughter of a military officer, and of a billionaire family no less," the Commissioner said.

"How's that possible? A billionaire officer, I mean."

"It's his wife's money and they're not what you'd expect. They live modestly on his salary while her fortune increases in investments. No condo on Manhattan's Billionaire Row. Just loving parents desperate to get their child back,"

"What happened?" I asked.

"They were in a supermarket. The child wandered the aisles while the mother's attention momentarily shifted and then she was gone. Store video shows her speaking to a man holding a toddler and a doll. The girl walks with him to a rear exit and vanishes. There's no camera out back."

What he said was reasonable. A young child is approached by a friendly man holding a toddler and doll. He asks for help and the child, entranced by the doll and possibility of making a new friend, accedes to his request, being too immature to grasp the world's potential dangers.

"When did this happen?" I asked.

"Yesterday evening."

"You don't have much time," I said.

Thanks to documentaries, even I knew that the countdown to finding a missing person alive begins the moment someone notifies the police. Investigators work against the clock with each passing hour decreasing the likelihood of the child's rescue and each passing minute decreasing the leads being found.

"Has a ransom note been received?" I asked.

"Not for money. The note which was messenger-delivered to her parents read, "It is God's will that many more children than your daughter will die."

Dead To Life

"*Many more...*" I said, slowly.
"Many more," the Commissioner repeated.

Chapter 101

"What can I do?" I asked.

"You wrote a paper with a fellow student in law school dealing with the interplay between state and federal courts," the Commissioner said.

Still troubled by the image of a kidnapped child, it took several moments for me to shift focus.

"Yes, I remember. Aimee Willkis, during our second year. I haven't seen her since though she might have been at the graduation ceremony which I skipped. She was smart but a bit weird too," I said.

"How so?" the Commissioner asked.

"Not with what she ever said but in her appearance: oddly dyed hair, once blue, and Goth makeup. Tattoos on her upper arm but thankfully not face or neck. They'd be a turnoff at law firms except maybe those with many media clients," I said, becoming uncomfortable as my speech began spilling.

"Do you know where she lives now?" he asked.

"Still near Columbia I expect, in a rent-controlled apartment inherited from her grandmother. We worked on the paper there. Why are you interested in her? I mean she *was* a bit strange, but..."

"Because of her involvement with our person-of-interest."

"Jorge?" I burst out.

"You know him?"

"Not really. He'd drop in when we were working. Eight-years older than her, elegantly dressed and drives a Maserati which got us into great restaurants when I went out with them," I said.

"Could you open contact with her now?" the Commissioner asked.

"I could think up some reason. An old school chum wanting to revisit memories, or maybe to get her ideas on decorating my new apartment. She has an artistic flair and was into such things," I said.

"Do it," the Commissioner said, before rising abruptly and leaving the restaurant.

April turned toward me.

"You've had your marching orders," she said.

Chapter 102

Finding Aimee wasn't hard since it was inconceivable that she would have moved. New York City rents are so outrageous that people would kill for her absurdly cheap rent-controlled apartment. Literally, not just figuratively. What would you do for a spacious, three-bedroom, well-located Manhattan apartment renting for seven-hundred-dollars a month? To be owned for your entire life and that of your heir too. Don't tell me. Deciding on my approach was harder.

Despite what I'd told the Commissioner, Aimee wasn't stupid or gullible. She'd had a hardscrabble childhood and was preternaturally suspicious. For me to suddenly turn up, all cheery and voluble, wouldn't do. What hook would gain her immediate trust?

April provided the answer.

"Bump into her and suggest something off-beat. Her boyfriend is unconventional so it could be in her nature. Say you're unsure what to do with your life. Since you both worked well together on the law paper, setting up a joint law practice would make sense. That the law firms you'd interviewed at were too white-shoe, too up-tight, places you'd be fired for farting. It's a good line and this approach might work. It sounds innocent enough."

And that's what we did. Waited across from her apartment, seated in April's car with tinted-windows. Watching until she appeared and noting the stores she entered. Meeting her at the local pizza restaurant seemed ideal.

Chapter 103

"Your ambush of Aimee must seem casual, there being a good reason why you entered that restaurant at that time. She'll naturally be suspicious, not having spoken with you for so long. New Yorkers are naturally distrustful and expect to be scammed, even when being asked for directions," April said.

"Telling a stranger directions can be risky?" I asked, feeling dumbfounded.

"That depends on who's asking. A friend told me he was approached by a woman on Thirtieth Street, asking if it would be alright if she asked for directions. When he agreed, she said she had a map in her purse, reached in, and pulled out a revolver which she thrust against his forehead, saying she would shoot him if he didn't give her his money. My friend saw the bullets in the cylinder and knew it was a real gun. He gave her the twenty-dollars in his pocket, always keeping his money, credit card, and driver's license in a hidden case worn around his neck. After she ran off, he reported the robbery to the police and was told his was the fourth such robbery in the area that day."

"That's some story," I said.

"Yes, so be careful."

"Always! My daddy taught me what to trust," I said, patting the pocket holding my pistol.

"Your loose pants conceals it well. Some women's pants are so tight you could see their religion," April said, in a serious tone.

I laughed and exited the car. The phrases she'd learned during her Down-South upbringing always amused me.

Chapter 104

Aimee was ordering at the counter when I entered the restaurant and took my place as third in line. I looked down at my phone so she would recognize me first.

"Well, Daisy, and don't you look all grown up," she said sprightly upon seeing me, clutching my arm and using the affectionate nickname she long before anointed me with. A character's name in a novel she loved in high school, she'd said.

"Aimee! Whatever are you doing now?" I squealed with feigned delight.

"Oh, this and that since graduation. I haven't yet decided. Too colorful for the firms I've interviewed at."

"I've had the same problem after being checked online which companies now do," I said.

"You *were* a media sensation."

"Not by choice. Kids don't choose the family they're born into," I said.

"That's a truism. But you've said that your father loved you," Aimee said.

"He did and it was why I did what I had to do," I said, speaking vaguely since the reality was still painful.

In the silence that followed, the counterman called her name.

"This is for my lunch and dinner. We can eat at my apartment," Aimee said.

I imagined April's satisfaction as she watched me chatting with Aimee outside the restaurant.

Chapter 105

Aimee's apartment was just as I'd remembered. Her grandmother's large, heavy, old-fashioned furniture remained with the only addition seeming her law school diploma which hung within an irreverent Disney character frame.

I felt at home seated at the Formica dining table, being reminded of the 1950s style kitchen at my grandmother's Bronx home. Stark white appliances contrasting with pastel hues of mint green and baby blue lent a light, airy feel to the room. I remembered the vintage canisters on open shelving and old-fashioned clock in the corner.

"You haven't changed anything," I said.

"No, I couldn't. It's grandma's and I still miss her. You must feel that too," Aimee said.

"My grandmother's alive and healthy," I said, ignoring her reference to my father.

"Is Roman still around?" she asked.

"Part of our family, always was, always will be," I said.

"An unusual family," she said, and I nodded.

She made coffee while I cut the pizza, a small slice for me and larger one for her, assuming that our appetites hadn't changed. We ate silently. I wanting her to set the tone and she apparently not knowing how to begin, old friendships not being easily picked up. Finally she spoke.

"You're at loose ends too," she said.

I simply nodded. Words had often been unneeded in the past since we could sense each other's thoughts.

"Maybe law was never right for me. My motive for studying it was emotional, not intellectual. I was mixed up for years," I said.

"I still am," Aimee said.

"You're more honest than me," I said with a smile.

Aimee's mood remained somber but thoughtful too.

"Did you ever consider a political career?" she asked.

"Never, considering my background," I said.

This silence was longer.

"My boyfriend, Jorge, will be here soon. He has some interesting ideas," she said in a matter-of-fact tone.

Chapter 106

Jorge didn't arrive until six and my five hours of improvisation during the wait came easy. Maybe I should have gotten a drama instead of law degree, I thought.

My "legend" came easy since Aimee's questions were the usual that I had long avoided from reporters. These concerned my father and presence at his execution.

"How could you bear going?" Aimee asked.

Her honestly surprised tone muddled my thinking. How could I? I *really* asked myself for the first time. The experience so molded and shadowed my life that I hadn't deeply considered it until her question. Having struggled to survive without thinking what was happening, like a swimmer who fears they'll drown if they note the size of the waves.

"I didn't really think about it until this moment. I told my grandmother that I wanted to see my father and she spoke with the lawyer. I hadn't fully realized that I would be viewing his execution, only that I would be his last visitor.

"When I left his cell the lawyer got cold feet. He said that my father deep down wouldn't want me there but I insisted. I said the court told me that I could and that I'd see he paid for it if he tried stopping me."

"He was probably more afraid of what you might tell your father's chums than anything you could do," Aimee said.

"You're right though at that moment if I had a gun and he tried to stop me I would have killed him. My dad was always there for me and now by God I would be there for him," I said venomously.

My tone caused Aimee to start and me to wonder: Where had my feelings been all these years?

Chapter 107

The next hours passed more comfortably, as if my confession eased things between us in some way. Returned us to the innocence of earlier school days though innocence had never been us. I because of who my father had been and she? I didn't know until that afternoon.

"I killed my brother, Billy, when I was fourteen," she suddenly blurted, and it might have been my calm lack of response which allowed her to continue.

"He was three and my mother asked me to babysit while she visited her sister who had walking pneumonia. I didn't want to, having a date with a boy trying hard to get to first base if you remember what that was. I told him I couldn't go out but that my mother wouldn't be home so he could come over."

I nodded understanding.

"I left my brother downstairs and my boyfriend came to my room. He'd just gotten his fingers inside me when I heard a crash but ignored it. You know what it's like."

I nodded again, hypnotized by her tone and dreading the finale of her story.

"Eventually, fearing my mother's arrival, I told him he had to leave and we fixed our clothes. Going downstairs I called 'Billy' but got no answer. I found him lying on the floor in the kitchen. He'd climbed on a chair, apparently to reach cookies in the middle of the table, fallen and banged his head on its corner. He lay bleeding on the floor as we pleasured ourselves. My parents never forgave me and I never forgave myself."

She sobbed and I touched her shoulder to comfort. Sisters, suffering together.

Chapter 108

"Neither of us could have acted differently. What happened was our fate, written in the stars long before we were born," I said.

Aimee looked up and, with a grimace that might have passed for a smile, touched my hand.

"You're a good friend. We shouldn't have lost contact," she said.

"You did well. Maybe you should have studied acting," Doctor Hess said years later.

"I wasn't acting. I don't know where that sentiment came from but felt it to be true," I said.

"There's some truth to it. A child is dependent on their parents and can't chart their own course. You're smart and would have excelled in school as you did but consider how your life would be had your parents been different. If rather than having a killer-for-hire father and absent mother they'd been an accountant and a homemaker."

"And what if they'd been a psychiatrist and a homemaker?" I asked cheekily.

Doctor Hess smiled.

"Well, then your life *might* have less painful. What followed with Aimee?" he asked.

"She showed me the changes she'd made in the apartment and new furnishings in what she called the guest bedroom. Said I should consider it mine and gave me a key to the apartment but added that I should text before coming. 'Jorge has a nervous trigger finger and I'm not joking,'" she explained.

"We spent the next hours watching her favorite TV series, *Blue Bloods*. She'd bought all its DVDs," I said.

"What did she like about the show?" Doctor Hess asked and I repeated her words as I remembered them,

"Did you watch it?" Aimee had asked me.

"No," I said.

"You'll love it. It's basically a modern-day Western set in New York City in which goodness vanquishes evil. But mostly because it's about a family. Every episode ends with their Sunday meal which begins with a prayer. An idyllic family gathering in which viewers partake."

"And like neither of us had," I said

A noise startled us and we looked up in Jorge's smiling face.

Chapter 109

It's hard to describe Jorge without sounding theatrical since his features were so disparate. Being tall and gaunt rather than thin but with the deep blue eyes and cleft chin that gave him movie star looks. Not like the typical matinee idol but more an erring son who couldn't be counted on to keep out of trouble. Of whom one continually asked even without evidence, "*What* did you do now?"

But Jorge was charming too. He would concentrate on the speaker, giving the impression they were the only people in the world. I understood his attraction for Aimee but not for me. His calculated manner reminded me of my father's friends.

Aimee introduced me as being more than a friend from law school. Saying that we like sisters since we struggled with the same issue of what to do in life.

"What would you like to do?" Jorge asked me.

"I'm not sure. Law school now seems like something I fell into, to keep me busy while growing up which I'm trying to do. I can't see myself surviving at the firms I interviewed. They're too vanilla and I'm..."

"Complicated?" Aimee suggested.

"That's a polite word for it," I said with a smile.

"Now I recognize you. I *though*t you familiar when I came in," Jorge said.

I froze, anticipating the usual frequent questions: "What did you feel when you saw it?" "What did you do after?"

"Yes, it's me," I said simply.

"It was probably terrible but you must have loved your father deeply," he said sympathetically.

"I did," I said, and felt surprised at the camaraderie I felt with Jorge, who was suspected of committing an unspeakable crime.

Chapter 110

While Jorge studied me I also studied him during the following three hours as I tried to behave like the confused post-graduate I pretended to be. Which he seemed to accept though I couldn't be sure. Nor could I be certain which of my replies to his questions found favor.

His initial questions were impersonal. "Where in the City do you live?" "Did you have a hard time finding the apartment?" "What were your law firm interviews like?"

Only after these did he reveal *his* personal life.

"I was born here but my parents came from Mexico. My father was killed while we visited his father. Shot before me when I was eight and I never really recovered from it. Did your father's death affect you the same?" he asked.

I noted the kindly way he phrased his question, speaking of my father's *death* rather than his *execution*.

"I guess. Even today I can't read about an execution, so phobic that if it's in a novel I instantly throw it out, unable to tolerate having it in the house."

"You got sick during the course on death penalty cases," Aimee blurted.

"I couldn't stay in the room. I'd feel hot and cold. My mouth would get dry and I was afraid I'd vomit. I left class early so many times that I was afraid I'd get a B," I said.

"You wound up all A's," Aimee said.

"Only after hustling the teacher with an apology. I told him I was pregnant and volunteered to help with research for the paper he was writing."

"You were pregnant?" Aimee asked with astonishment.

"In my story I was," I said.

I was pleased they laughed at this deception but couldn't help wondering if my present act held.

Chapter 111

The pizza that Aimee brought home was great though not a good-enough meal for Jorge. It not being Mexican food seemed to affect his sensibility and we went out.

The elegance of his Maserati Quattroporte impressed me: the three-blade design of its signature air ducts, boomerang shaped rear lights, and keyless entry and soft close door. I could afford to buy one but aren't a car person.

Jorge drove carefully, letting other cars cut him off to which his only reaction was a softly muttered Spanish curse that he didn't bother translating.

The Times Square restaurant was comfortable, having great food, service, and atmosphere. Here there was no worry for this semi-vegetarian. Each dish had its ingredients listed on the menu with vegetables, grains, and fish seeming a staple of Mexican meals. The restaurant's Vegetarian Friendly and Vegan options made my choice a breeze.

As main dish I chose Salmon Zarandeado which was grilled salmon, Veracruz sauce, tomatoes, olives, capers, and Spanish Rice. Jorge ordered Oaxacan Shrimp Quesadilla which was tortilla, shrimp, Mexican cheeses, smoked mushrooms, and tomatoes. I don't remember what Aimee ordered.

For dessert I forgot about healthy eating and gorged on Dark Chocolate Tamal which is warm molten chocolate cake, chocolate sauce, and vanilla ice cream.

"Breaking your diet?" Aimee asked, with a grin, remembering my school days' eating habit.

"It's all so good," I gushed, and Jorge smiled.

That statement wasn't acting!

Chapter 112

"So much was written about your father. What was he *really* like?" Jorge asked.

His question hit me like a blow, finding me unprepared with no prepared script. So I improvised, or was what I said really true I later asked myself.

"The news reports didn't describe the man I knew," I began.

"Only one's family knows them best," Jorge murmured empathetically.

I nodded agreement and continued.

"It was growing up in his neighborhood which created him. That and the military's training made him a killer though his victims deserved it. He knew the risks of being in the life and accepted them. He loved books and encouraged me to read. Once, when in prison, it saved his life," I said.

"How?" Aimee asked excitedly and Jorge's interest perked.

"He'd been sentenced to three-years. Never told me why only said he'd been young and naive. On the bus taking him to prison he sat next to Gene, an old-timer with many arrests for burglary and prison having become a second home for him. Gene took a liking to my father and told him how to survive 'inside.' To not ask questions of other inmates and try getting a desirable job in the library or kitchen. Talking religion with the visiting parish priest would help too.

"Gene had a fifty-dollar bill in each shoe which he slipped to guards who knew him from before. They arranged for my father to share Gene's cell, and Gene told him what to tell the warden who interviewed all new prisoners. Thanks to his advice my father *was* made a library clerk but only after spending two-months mopping floors. Gene worked in the kitchen and gave my dad heaping plates.

"My dad returned the favors. Gene was small and disliked by another con for some reason. My dad passed the word that anyone who laid a hand on Gene would 'eat his prick the next day,' and Gene was never touched."

"That's some story," Aimee said.

"My father was some man," I said, and cried.

Chapter 113

I never know how to behave when a person starts crying. Nor, I think, do most people. But letting me cry it out seemed best, which was what Jorge and Aimee did since I felt better afterward.

"You seemed to need that," Jorge said.

"I did. I never cry," I said.

"I was that way for a long time," he said.

"What caused you to change?" Aimee asked.

"Stomach pains," Jorge said with a smile.

"The doctor told me feelings can't be repressed. That if one tries, they'll be expressed through the body in symptoms like my stomach pains. So I let myself cry when the feeling came and the pains went away. He gave good advice," Jorge said.

"That was good acting," the Commissioner told me later.

"It wasn't an act. I cried because I loved my father and could tolerate his execution only by killing part of me. I guess it was time for that part to come out," I said.

The Commissioner nodded.

"What happened next with them?" he asked.

"Talk about casual things. My last job interview during which my breasts were ogled, and Aimee's which ended almost before it began once they saw her tattoos. Me being too straight and she being too raunchy, I guess."

"Did Jorge make a pass at you?" the Commissioner asked.

"No, not at all and I would have noticed. He was more like an older brother," I said.

"You liked him," the Commissioner said.

"I did."

"Just remember that he might he a killer."

"I'm used to them," I said cheekily.

The Commissioner stared as his phone rang.

Chapter 114

Though curious, it would have been impolite to listen openly as the Commissioner spoke so I deliberately looked about the room. On the wall hung a portrait of President Theodore Roosevelt when he'd been Police Commissioner. The present Commissioner was a handsome man and I wondered about his wife, not that I considered trying to seduce him.

When the phone call ended he looked away for a few moments before rising from his chair and speaking quickly.

"There was a terror attack in Grand Central Station with many deaths. Keep up the good work," he said, before hurriedly leaving.

I'd been too young for the terror attack on the World Trade Centers to affect me but relatives told me the aftermath. Posted photos of missing loved ones and the memorial at Judson Church. Of crying people wandering the streets, others rushing to help at the bombed site and the increase of gun sales. Events that felt like ancient history until now when my world seemed to shift.

I'd thought of going to Grand Central Station but my assignment was to save a child and prevent future carnage. Was she somehow involved in today's attack? I need wait to learn, as would the rest of the nation.

The uproar at One Police Plaza disappeared when I reached the street. There, things looked normal as I sought a coffee shop to relax before events overtook me too. Being several blocks from the commercial bustle of Chinatown, finding one didn't take long.

Chapter 115

The coffee shop lacked Chinese aura with its Italian name and Western selections. But it was close by and I felt worn-out. Acting is hard when lives are at stake: the young girl's, and mine if Jorge became suspicious. If he was who the Commissioner suspected, which wasn't yet certain.

The store was tiny and the seats of uncushioned wood but the breads were extraordinary. So, despite my dieting fetish, I sipped latte while nibbling on almond and halvah croissants. Staring at but restraining myself from the chocolate babka. Feeling better afterward since eating lessens anxiety.

Customers stared at the TV in the corner while awaiting their orders. Few people remained after receiving them, likely hurrying to the protection of home though being close to the safety of Police Headquarters. My table was empty except for me and a well-dressed man who soon turned toward me.

"It's a scary time. The place is usually packed with customers hanging-out. Now everyone is anxious to get home," he said.

"Home is where the heart is," I said.

The trite saying seemed appropriate.

"Why aren't you going home?" he asked.

Though not usually sharing personal information with strangers this was a strange time.

"I live alone. I guess I don't want to be alone just now," I said.

"Living alone isn't good. I had a wife and child," he said.

"Had?" I asked, puzzled by his use of past tense since he wasn't yet out of his twenties.

"My wife was murdered two-months ago and our child now lives with her grandparents," he said hesitantly, his voice catching.

Chapter 116

"That's terrible. What happened?" I asked.

"You missed the news. It was a big story," he said.

"I was in law school. Study took all my time," I said.

"Our fifteen-year-old neighbor spent a year in a juvenile reformatory after threatening my wife and beating our daughter. The day after his release he broke into his father's gun cabinet, took a shotgun, and blew off my wife's head. After that he killed himself. Thankfully he spared our daughter."

"What idiot released him?" I asked.

"I'm looking for a lawyer so maybe we'll learn. But no amount of money will bring her back."

"No. None is ever 'ready' for the death of a loved one," I said.

The sadness of my tone struck him and he stared at my face.

"You're her, aren't you?"

I nodded.

"How could you, being so young," he said.

"He was my father and I loved him. A person will do many things for love and he wasn't all bad," I said simply.

"One never gets the whole story in the news," he said.

Again, I simply nodded.

"Can I accompany you home? For protection, just in case," he added.

"Or me to protect you," I said, opening my carry bag to reveal my pistol.

"It's legal. I have a carry-permit," I said quickly.

He nodded and made a slight smile as we rose to leave the cafe.

"You may be just the atypical lawyer I'm looking for," he said.

Chapter 117

He hailed a taxi and gave an address west of mine, close by the Hudson River.

Tilden was his name, one that had been passed through generations ever since his originating family came off the Mayflower.

"My mother belongs to the DAR, Daughters Of The American Revolution," he said with a smile.

"Mine waited for the steamship to Ellis Island," I said, to indicate my feelings about pedigree.

"It means nothing to me either," he said.

At his building's entrance he invited me in and I accepted, still feeling worn-out.

"Being your armed protection it's necessary for me to accompany you to your door," I said in a mock serious tone. Acting seemed to be becoming a habit with me.

We both smiled at my jest.

I remarked that his fourteenth-floor apartment would have gorgeous views of the Hudson River and New Jersey were it not surrounded by taller buildings.

"I bought it before they built them," he said, pointing out the window. "But it has a fitness center and it's a short walk to the subway to work," he added.

"What do you do?" I asked.

"Consulting and teaching computer science at Columbia's engineering school," he said.

"Manhattan is a tough place to live," I said, sympathetically.

"What's your apartment like," he asked.

"I share a three-bedroom with two roommates. We've just moved in so we'll see. My grandmother lives in the Bronx and I go home regularly.

"Your apartment isn't your home?" he asked perceptively.

175

"Home is where the heart is," I said, repeating this trite phrase to not reveal more.

He turned on the mammoth sixty-five-inch TV and tuned to the news. The video showed three shooters wearing COVID masks and entering Grand Central Station. Once inside they removed short-barreled rifles and shotguns from shopping bags. Then shot indiscriminately at adults and children before exiting, one through one exit and two through another, apparently to distinguish them from the shooters during the ensuing melee, to make them appear fleeing potential victims. Engrossed in watching the video, I hadn't noticed Tilden's presence with a tray.

"Sickening, isn't it?" he said, rhetorically.

I could only nod.

Chapter 118

We quietly sipped the coffee that Tilden prepared.

"You look depressed," he said.

"I am. First your story and now this," I said.

"I'm sorry. I shouldn't have told you," he said.

"No, it's alright. It's an important part of your life and you must have sensed I would understand," I said.

"Your life story is just as difficult," he said.

We sat silently for a while, watching the video of survivor interviews.

"I've been depressed since it happened. The information my therapist gave me helped. He said depression is a *depressing* of feelings and I did feel better after crying. My daughter needs me too and I must be strong for her," Tilden said.

It was several moments before I spoke.

"I've probably been depressed all my life. From my mother's desertion and later my father's... But I had support too. My lawyer was always there and so was my grandmother and Roman," I said.

"Is Roman your brother?" Tilden asked.

"Not quite," I said, unable to keep from smiling.

"He's lived with us since I was a toddler. He's six-years younger than my father, has no family and sort of adopted ours as we did him. He was my father's bodyguard and you could say he's my combination bodyguard, brother, and father. Nothing will save anyone that he fears is a danger to me," I said.

"You had quite a family," Tilden said.

"One can't choose the family they're born into but I wouldn't have chosen another. It made me who I am," I said.

Tilden looked thoughtful before speaking.

"You *are* the lawyer I've been looking for," he said firmly.

Chapter 119

We spoke for another hour before I left. Mostly about his prospective case: to gain financial compensation for his wife's murder and loss, which was all that could be obtained. I said he need sign a contract authorizing me as his counsel, and that my fee would be thirty-per-cent of what was awarded and nothing if we lost.

"That seems reasonable," he said.

Only after leaving did I realize what I'd promised: to pursue a lawsuit without an office or staff. Then another idea hit me. That were Aimee my partner I would have a perfect reason for our continuing contact, likely seeing her almost daily. Moreover, despite her startling makeup and flakiness, she'd also been an "A" student in law school and would be a good partner with her fury at what happened to Tilden's wife being as strong as mine.

I phoned her immediately after leaving Tilden's apartment and said she had to meet me.

"What's wrong? Aren't you well?" she asked with concern.

Her warmth increased the belief that I'd made the right decision.

"I'm fine. I was just offered a million-dollar case and want you as my partner in our new practice. We'll only take cases we like and won't take shit from anyone," I said firmly.

"It sounds like Heaven," Aimee said with a laugh. "Come over. Jorge's here and he might have good ideas."

Meeting Tilden in Chinatown had produced a favorable development. The Commissioner would be pleased and might know someone who would rent us impressive office space too.

Chapter 120

Immediately after speaking with Aimee I phoned the Commissioner and asked that we meet.

"For good or bad news?" he quickly asked.

"Very good. You'll be pleased but I need your help," I said.

"I can use good news today," he said.

"How many are dead?" I asked.

"Sixteen with seven on the critical list and many with bruises and trauma. Their lives will never be the same."

"No," I said, being no stranger to trauma.

"I have an uptown meeting scheduled and we can meet in my car. It's a Black Lincoln town car and will be parked on Beekman Place in an hour, that's between 50th and 51st Streets. Two-blocks of affluent peace, deserted except for a few passersby.

"I'll be there," I said.

Being instinctively prompt, I arrived at the location with twenty-minutes to spare and walked the area. It was as he said: ghost-town quiet except for the occasional hurrying pedestrian and doormen who ignored me. The Commissioner's car parked and I quickly slipped into the back seat.

"What's so important?" he asked brusquely.

I described my accidental meeting with Tilden, the murder of his wife and lawsuit I was hired to pursue. He seemed uninterested until learning of Aimee's involvement.

"It's a great reason to deepen your friendship with the two of them," he said.

"That's what I thought but I need your help. Pursuing a legal case requires an office which we don't have. Do you know a lawyer who would rent me attractive space? Not a hole-in-the-wall but something to give Tilden confidence in the novice he hired," I said.

"That's easily solved and the best problem I was handed today. I'm pleased and don't doubt that Tilden and I made the right choice," he said.

He moved to hug me before restraining himself.

"You're busy. I'll get going," I said.

"You're dealing with a viper, take care" he said.

"Always," I replied.

Chapter 121

The Commissioner phoned next morning.

"I've found an impressive law office for you. A partner is my old friend so he won't charge. Call him," he said, and I did..

Hamilton, which how he insisted I address him, scheduled our meeting for the afternoon. That his name reflected Tilden's old English lineage seemed a bit of luck, which I hoped to increase by dressing right.

A survival fact that I learned in law school is that seventy-five-percent of people form their first impression of a lawyer based on appearance, whether it's professional enough. And that it is particularly important for women lawyers who should appear serious but not sexy.

Women were advised to wear a black, gray, or navy tailored skirt or pantsuit and low-heeled polished shoes. The blouse should not be too tight, comfortable to wear, and of a fabric that will look crisp during a long working day.

Jewelry should be simple, like a minimalist watch, to not detract from the seriousness of meetings or court proceedings, with flashy items seeming especially disrespectful for a woman lawyer. A classic leather black or brown briefcase, for carrying electronics or documents, also reflects professionalism. All would be critical to gaining Tilden's trust and Hamilton's good opinion.

Hamilton's law firm was impressive as was its history with an ancestry deriving from before the Civil War. Located on two floors of a Madison Avenue skyscraper it had a winding wooden staircase between them.

The office he led me to was also impressive having large wood furniture, Oriental carpeting, and a view of the East River. While drinking their excellent tea, I quickly described my problem.

"Will this be satisfactory?" he asked, with a smile.

"Nore than that," I almost gushed.

"It's yours," he said, with another smile.

"How can I repay you?" I asked, feeling indebted.

"You already have. Your father once saved my life," he said.

His response shocked me and I barely kept from crying as I asked, "How?"

Chapter 122

After telling Doctor Hess of my tearfulness upon learning that my father had saved Hamilton's life, he said this explained much about mine. That to survive I had to *compartmentalize*, place people in psychological boxes separate from my feelings to tolerate my family's stresses.

"Sensing your father's profession and unable to bear it, you placed his image in an unopened box, one that newly learned facts are only now opening. Despite his numerous killings, though admittedly of criminals, he's considered a hero by important people. This is demolishing the unconscious unbearable conclusions you created as barrier between your feelings and your intellect, created in early childhood and keeping you isolated."

I didn't argue since I sensed he was right. And one tends not to dispute their analyst apart from practical matters like appointment times or turning up the air conditioner. But mostly because I'd begun to experience what I felt was a splitting of my consciousness that enabled me to see things more broadly.

"Your father was a complex man," Doctor Hess concluded.

"Aren't we all?" I asked cheekily, feeling grateful for his assessment but also anger from the anxiety it aroused.

"Some more than others," he said.

"I just had a crazy thought," I said.

Doctor Hess waited.

"That the woman who I believe is my mother wasn't."

"What causes you to think that?"

"Something I overheard my grandmother say when I was a child."

"Which was?"

Dead To Life

"She said, 'If Katrina hadn't died you'd never have married that Swedish whore. What made you think she could be a mother?'"

Chapter 123

"*This* is *our* office?" Aimee exclaimed upon seeing it.

"Only the best for our firm," I said, tongue-in-cheek.

"*Right*! Who did you..."

My deadly look shut her up before she completed the insult.

"It's a favor from a friend," I said cryptically.

She stared but closed the subject and we spent the rest of the day getting organized. Which required little effort apart from arranging for the printing of letterhead and business cards. Hamilton had assigned us a secretary and we had only to meet with our one client and cope with our anxieties. Which were many since the tiniest lawyer error can be disastrous. As I explained to Tilden, after our secretary served coffee and he looked about the room.

"Your office is impressive," he said.

I nodded without replying as if it were normal for us, remembering that image is everything.

"There's a rigid procedure when filing a lawsuit for damages which I'll explain. One can only sue if they have *standing*, which means they were harmed by the defendant against whom the claim is made with the remedy being financial. Your wife can't be returned to you but..."

Tilden teared and I waited a moment before continuing.

"We must identify all possible defendants, which in your case means the institution and doctors involved in releasing the murdering teenager. The more defendants identified, the greater will be compensation for your pain and to ensure your daughter's future.

"The correct court must be chosen which, with your case, will be New York State since this is where the event happened and the claim thus arose. Suit must also be filed within deadline by filing the proper court documents which are a civil cover sheet, a summons, and a complaint, which are served on the defendant.

"They will submit counter-claims and there will be pre-trial conferences to address major issues in the case. Discovery will follow during which evidence will be exchanged and a date set for trial," I explained.

"When will that be?" Tilden asked.

"Possibly never. Many civil cases are settled out of court with an agreed financial remedy in exchange for waiving further claim. They'll probably offer a settlement which you must decide if adequate," I said.

"No amount of money can make up for losing my wife," Tilden exclaimed.

Though nodding, my mind was elsewhere, wondering if I would ever love so deeply.

Chapter 124

I worked mechanically over the following days, my mind in a whirl from what I'd learned. That my father had been valued by important people and my biological mother could be other than who I believed. *Now* my life began to make sense, giving me hope for the future. So that, maybe one day, I might gain the storied life I'd read of and envied. One with a loving husband and child though being willing to skip the house with picket fence, having learned that apartment living could be fine so long as it was spacious, had well-functioning appliances and a responsive maintenance staff.

I also learned that I was a competent attorney, feeling increasingly confident in knowing what needed doing and how. The information that I provided Tilden hadn't been feigned, just to project image.

Surprisingly, though a newcomer I quickly became considered a member of the law firm's staff and prey to their gossip. Which was comforting as my legal work progressed and I learned more about the murder of Tilden's wife.

He tearily described hearing of her death from the police, his notification of relatives and formal identification of her body. Which, because of the severity of her facial and bodily injuries, seemed superfluous, there being no tattoo or the like. After that painful meeting the office gossip provided a welcome distraction and I perked up upon overhearing a secretary's comment: "I feel guilty liking to come to work so much. When my husband goes shopping at Trader Joe's I sometimes think he should stay there."

Chapter 125

Is this what married life is like, I wondered, and moved closer to the conversation.

"My root-canal yesterday was my special alone time," Janet said.

I couldn't help laughing and they drew me into their circle.

"What's your marriage like?" Janet asked.

"I'm not," I said.

"Your relationship then?" she pressed.

Apparently my life was to be their morning's escape from the travails of work and family.

"Minimal compared to yours. Overnights with a guy that I like who's eligible but without commitment. What's now called a friendship with benefits," I said.

"But you do like him?" Melody asked.

"I wouldn't have slept with him if I didn't," I said.

"So what's holding up the ceremony if he's eligible," Janet asked.

"It may be the twenty-first century but women still don't do the proposing," I said.

"I did," Melody said.

Both Janet and I stared.

"Well, sort of," Melody corrected. "My parents returned early from vacation and found us in their bed."

"So?" I asked.

"My dad is bigger than my husband and our family is Italian. They tend to be emotional, my father is sort of connected and my husband was scared. He squeaked, 'We're getting married,' and did. You understand. You're Italian too," she said to me.

"And your father..." Melody added, knowingly.

I nodded without replying, wondering if I'd ever lose my unwanted media fame.

Chapter 126

Listening to their gossip served to establish our friendship. Not a real friendship as can develop between fellow students and neighbors but of the office variety. Daily contact during which the anxieties of work and family are shared. Though sometimes one loses it and breaks the unspoken rule against sharing too personal a matter. Then others listen without commenting, providing supportive shoulder when something becomes too much. Which never happened to me. Keeping secrets, both family and personal, was a rule that I gained in childhood and never broke.

"Holding this attitude makes closeness difficult," Doctor Hess had said.

"Which explains my isolation, doesn't it?" I asked rhetorically.

But there *was* one friend, Rhoda, with whom I shared *some* things. Her family moved next door when we were in second grade. One day I sat outside with my grandmother when she and her mother sat outside their house. Rhoda said 'hello,' I responded, and our friendship began. She carried the same book I was reading, "Clara and the Bookwagon," a historical fiction taking place in 1905. Clara hungers to attend school but must work on the family farm to help with chores and her younger siblings. The new town librarian will use a wagon to bring books to families who can't get to the library and Clara hopes to persuade her father to let her learn to read.

"Perhaps like you wanted someone to bring you into the larger world apart from your family," Doctor Hess had interpreted.

"I guess, probably. They moved four years later and I never saw Rhoda again," I said.

Dead To Life

My office friendships weren't deep. Rhoda and I had shared real feelings as much as young children can. But with my office buddies I was only a hanger-on.

Chapter 127

It felt good being part of a group, the instinct to run to cliques being settled in every female's breast at birth. And here, because the work of lawyers often demonstrates human frailties, the gossip can be delicious. Both Melody and Janet smiled as I joined them.

"You'll *never* believe lawyers would do this," Melody exclaimed.

"Then I certainly would," I said, and smiled.

"The client's problem, video of her having sex, is becoming common," Melody said.

"She violated the Eleventh Commandment: Don't take off your clothes in front of a camera. It should be tattooed on every kid," I said.

"You got it. But it isn't about her but what happened with lawyers at their impromptu stag party," she said, and my ears perked up.

"This CEO'S college-student daughter sued her boyfriend for making a video of their intimate moments which he showed his fraternity brothers. The incident became widely known, forcing her to withdraw from college. Despite the girl's hesitancy, her mother insisted on suing the boy and the video was placed in evidence. Wanting to keep it out of circulation, the girl's lawyer asked the judge to order it wouldn't be shared with opposing counsel but the judge refused, stating that lawyers could be trusted.

"*Really,*" I said cynically, already knowing what happened.

"Yep, not only did the lawyer watch it when preparing his appeal but nineteen other staff members did with one saying, 'Let's get to the good part.' That law firm is now being sued and the original six-figure damages demand has turned into a seven-figure one."

Dead To Life

"I hope she wins," I said.

Chapter 128

"I'm surprised that one of that firm's lawyer's didn't complain," Melody said.

"That can kill a career. I learned this in law school though I'm not sure if the example was intended as a moral or cautionary lesson," I said and moved closer.

"A New York lawyer who I'll call Jones believed the lawyer his firm assigned to handle his home sale closing behaved unethically and should be reported to the state disciplinary authorities as required by the Code of Professional Responsibility. Instead, the firm fired Jones even though the offending lawyer admitted the charge was correct. Jones sued for wrongful discharge with his case winding its way for years through courts at great expense. When it was publicized in a legal magazine, he was fired from his latest job as corporate executive. It takes a Don Quixote to protest, a person who's willing to buck the establishment for nearly a lifetime."

"Or maybe an angel," Melody said.

I nodded agreement, hoping that my first case would have a better end.

These relaxing moments ended with the phone call from Thomas, which a more experienced woman than me would have expected. Even a teenager knows that the way to keep a boyfriend is to have sex with them. Which I did enjoy though not deciding what I wanted: a comforting occasional bedmate, a husband, or simply to create the memory of enjoyable moments. My vague response reflected this.

"I miss you," he said.

"I'm sorry but I've been dealing with so many things: my new apartment and setting up an office to handle the case that fell into my lap. I've hardly had time to breathe," I apologized.

"You need a back rub."

"I need a vacation," I said.

"Come over tonight."

"My grandmother complained she's feeling badly. It could be just wanting to see me but I promised I'd be home tonight. My roommate is giving a party Saturday night. Come over my place then," I suggested.

He said he would and I gave him the address.

"You don't seem anxious to see him," Melody said, having overheard.

"He's nice but I don't know what I want," I said.

"Men can do that to you," she said.

Chapter 129

Learning the office secrets was a mixed blessing, granting intimacy but also the responsibility for what knowing entails. Adding to yet another of those I carried.

All but one was known by the Commissioner. Not from lack of trust but because I couldn't fathom his reaction were he to learn, or mine were I to focus on my liking of Jorge. Not as a potential bedmate but a fellow sufferer, the product of an equally disastrous childhood who struggled to survive in the world.

But drug lords did horrendous deeds and I knew what might happen. After arrest, Jorge could be tortured by the Mexican police and maybe Aimee too if arrested with him. Both outcomes were certainly possible. To paraphrase Napoleon: *Fate is accident misnamed,* and who could have predicted any of our lives?

A stomach cramp hit me, my second that day, and I had felt unusually tired on recent days. Early in my psychotherapy, Doctor Hess told me that stress could create symptoms mimicking nearly every medical disorder. So, considering all that I was struggling with, I believed this was its cause until mentioning my distress to Melody. Her comment sent my heart racing.

"Maybe you're pregnant," she said.

Chapter 130

Young girls mother their dolls as precursor to motherhood. Playing at being married is also common. I never did either though whether from my family's oddness or mine is a moot question.

So my initial response to possibly being pregnant was both panic and bewilderment. Thomas had been my only lover and he'd worn a condom, a contraceptive method that I had believed foolproof. But Google now told me it wasn't, having a failure rate of fourteen-percent. Great odds for New York's lottery but not the Lottery of Life. Whether I could be a good mother wasn't the issue. Having the right time for it was and this wasn't it.

"Have you tested?" Melody asked, interrupting my reverie.

"No, I'd better," I said.

Investigating online, I learned that all brands worked the same with the key suggestions being to make sure the test wasn't expired and to wait until you missed your period. I bought the First Response Early Result Pregnancy Test which boasted ninety-seven-percent accuracy and an ergonomically designed handle making it easy to use without having to pee into a cup. A week later, after holding the stick in my first-morning's urine, I found I wasn't pregnant. Repeating the test on the following two days gained the same conclusion, and relief!

Chapter 131

I returned to work with a vengeance and none too soon. Both Tilden and the Commissioner had left messages, demanding to know what was happening. With both I was suave but honest, stressing the difficulty, what I'd accomplished, and insisting I was hard at work.

I told Tilden that the formal complaint had been filed with the court and all defendants served notice of the lawsuit. That they had filed their responses, admitting or denying blame, and discovery would follow with evidence being exchanged. All was happening, with the date of deposition being arranged of which he would be notified.

My talk with the Commissioner was vaguer. I said I'd become closer with both Jorge and Aimee, speaking with Aimee daily at work and mingling with them two to three times a week. That I was having dinner with them that evening to which Jorge would be bringing friends and I would keep him informed.

"I knew you could do it," the Commissioner said, supportively.

Okay, but what if they're suspicious? I thought but didn't say.

The rest of the day was spent preparing for the next afternoon's pretrial conference with the judge to discuss the particulars of the case. Despite Aimee's flakiness, she was a good partner and we both worked hard and felt confident, our biggest professional concern before leaving the office that evening being what to wear to court. Wanting our clothes to reflect seriousness and signal the gravity with which we regarded the legal system.

We would wear conservative, understated clothes, a dress or pantsuit with closed-toe shoes. Aimee's tattoos must be concealed as much as possible and her facial piercings removed. My insistence of this hurt her feelings but client interests come first.

Chapter 132

Aimee dropped a large envelope on my desk as we were leaving for the judge's chambers.

"This is addressed to you. The receptionist gave it to me," she said.

It was one of the Post Office's red/white/blue Priority Mail envelopes. I stared as it lay atop the piled mail on the antique wood desk. The name on the return address seemed familiar but I couldn't immediately place it. Memories can be strange, occasionally popping up to deliver their unwanted message of loss and taking the person unaware, freezing them back into the past.

"Are you alright?" Aimee asked.

"Yes, just thinking," I said hurriedly, trying to regain composure after remembering. Karl, the person sending the envelope, was the kindly prison guard who had attended my father before his execution. He had always held my hand as we walked to my father's cell during visits, speaking of his daughter my age to calm me. He had tried to approach me as I left the prison but was prevented by the crowd of reporters. I could still picture his sad face a dozen years later. Why had he contacted me *now*?

"We have to get going," Aimee said, ending my reverie.

I thrust the envelope into the briefcase holding papers for the judicial conference. I would open it later. Whatever matter lay dormant for so long could wait a few more hours, I thought.

Aimee held my hand tightly as we left the office, as if sensing my upset, that I wasn't all there.

Chapter 133

Though being my first paid legal experience, I knew what to do, both law school and legal internship having prepared me well. Papers were exchanged, assertions and denials made, and the order for discovery was gained. Participants left the judge's chambers in the customary friendly fashion. All was business, nothing personal.

Though enticed by the cuticles of memory and a shapeless hunger to open the envelope, my client needed support. Thus we lunched with Tilden and listened, which is often the best support.

Why had Karl sent me the letter *now*, long after the traumatic event? Would its information paralyze me again, or finally free me from my past though never of love for my father. And was my hope for freedom an inspiration or delusion, a never to be attained goal.

Would the letter reveal my father as a lost soul wandering a depressed landscape in the darkness of night, or someone greater? The heroic figure which the Commissioner and Hamilson's words teased but would I ever know.

"You seemed distracted," Aimee said after we bid farewell to Tilden.

Telling the truth is sometimes best, I thought as I replied.

"I just got a letter about my father," I said.

"He was executed a dozen years ago," Aimee insisted and stared.

"It was just sent by his prison guard. I don't know why he so delayed. Maybe I'll learn," I said.

"I can't wait to hear," Aimee said excitedly.

"No, I must read it alone," I said.

The silence between us hung heavy until Aimee spoke.

"I understand. But I'm here if you need me," she said softly and touched my arm.

Chapter 134

"What did the letter say?" Doctor Hess had asked.

"Everything and nothing," I replied cryptically.

It was a too private matter and one that I didn't relish speaking of, like describing your period to a man.

Doctor Hess had waited, not changing the subject as I hoped, so I read it to him from a copy, the original being locked in my safety deposit box until I decided its fate. Whether to destroy it or bequeath it to my children after my murder, which my father had feared.

"Dearest Annika,

"My life will soon be over without seeing you grown and established. But fate intervened so it must be your grandmother and Roman who safeguard your future.

"Because this letter will be painful to read I have asked Karl to deliver it unopened to you once your life is established as an adult. He is a good man and I trust he will.

"To ease your mind concerning my execution I now admit my guilt. I did commit murder, which is a sin, though my victims were evil. Lawful means could not end their reign of destruction and other ways were needed. It is fitting that the means they used to maintain their power was used to bring them down.

"I was not alone in this endeavor but will not identify the others. Vengeance has a long arm but they have promised to protect you and may have already contacted you by the time you receive my letter.

"My remaining secret, that of your mother, I intended to inform you and keeping it secret for so long may have been a mistake. Your biological mother, Katrina, did not die during childbirth but lives. After your birth, wanting to shield you from my chosen life, we exchanged ultimatum: hers was that she would leave if I didn't end my work and mine was that she would never separate you from me. Fearing my nature she left, leaving me with the guilt that remains. I trust you will find her and, if there is a merciful God, He protect you both."

I lay down the letter and sobbed.

Chapter 135

It was a glorious sunny day but I didn't notice as the taxi had dropped me off at Doctor Hess' office, having told Aimee that I would meet her later for dinner with Jorge. What my father's letter revealed had made me feel and I still had my task for the Commissioner too.

I'd felt disconnected, psychically lost after reading it. As perhaps had my father, holding his secrets without family support. Living behind a wall of misunderstandings that he built and couldn't escape, absorbed in contributing value to the society that despised him.

"Your father was a complex man," Doctor Hess said as I reached for Kleenex.

"That's putting it mildly," I said.

"And a heroic figure if what he said was true."

"Do analysts trust anyone?" I asked angrily.

"Analysts trust verified facts and believe the unconscious is powerful. Do you have any verified information that what he wrote is true," he said in an even tone.

This I hadn't considered. That the letter might be fantasy, intended to improve my image of my publicly condemned father and make my painful notoriety easier to bear.

Silence hung heavily between us. I couldn't share that both the Police Commissioner and a prominent lawyer had hinted of my father's goodness. A secret is secret only so long as it remains unspoken. Then I remembered a puzzling incident which I could relate.

"There is something. Once, while at law school, I was walking along Riverside Drive a block from Riverside Church, Two men suddenly appeared and while one held my mouth the other tried to force me into a car. Moments later a huge man clubbed them and grabbed me away. They fled, my savior released me and said, "You have stout friends but take greater care." Then he too disappeared. A week later I received a registered letter containing a pistol permit and list of firearms instructors. It said my application to carry a concealed weapon had been approved but I'd never applied for it," I said.

"You're packing?" Doctor Hess asked warily.

"Ever since then. A gun is like toilet paper, when you need it you need it bad. My concealed-carry vest holds wallet and keys too. I own four vests in different patterns and colors. They're functional and cute," I said.

For once Doctor Hess was speechless.

Chapter 136

I felt better after that therapy session. It more resembled being with a friend than a doctor and I'd needed someone to share the trauma of my father's letter, having none other than Doctor Hess to trust with its contents. Yet that session also marked a change in my treatment, reflecting my assertiveness in revealing being armed and Doctor Hess' unease with it. Would he feel the same were I a man? I wondered.

So, at the end of that session, I told him that I was stopping therapy though whether temporarily or permanently I didn't know. To my surprise he agreed, saying that I was no longer the desperate teenager who first arrived at his office and that he expected to hear good things of my life.

"It won't be good if you hear about me. My goal is to become anonymous," I said with a grin.

"No, it'll be good. We've spoken for a long time and you can always tell a winner at the starting gate," he said.

"A winner and a loser," I said, and he smiled.

"Do stay safe and consider me a friend. I'm here if you ever need an ear," he said.

After rising from the sofa I moved to hug goodbye but he raised his hands in mock horror.

"Can't touch. It could get me into trouble," he said with a smile.

Physical contact is forbidden between patient and analyst.

While traveling home to change for the dinner with Aimee and Jorge I felt a surge of confidence. Beginning analysis had been a sound decision as was ending it now.

Chapter 137

Jorge said dinner would be late as is typical in Latin countries. So, feeling worn-out, I napped before going and it did the trick. Upon opening my eyes I was in a good mood, cheerful and serene. What one usually feels before fully awakening to face a disagreeable task of the day. A burden that you can't quite remember but you know will occur to you in a moment. What hung over my head since my talk with the Commissioner: the life of the kidnapped child and maybe more horrors to come. And the day goes on.

"It's the throne of New York's Mexican cuisine," Jorge said as we entered the car. An Uber tonight since his Maserati was being repaired. "Stained upholstery," he explained, and I couldn't help wondering if it was from blood.

Scanning the restaurant's menu relieved the tension I feel when eating out, a painful indulgence for a semi-vegetarian like me and worse for an orthodox Vegan. But Jorge had understood.

"There are Vegan dishes too," he said, obviously proud at remembering my need.

Is Jorge *really* the monster being sought? I wondered again.

Sharing dishes wasn't Aimee's or Jorge's style so I was saved from refusing *that* ritual which I disliked, and there was much on the menu I liked. Whatever Jorge's faults he had impeccable taste.

The day's tumultuous happenings wiped out my appetite so I just noshed on vegetarian fare: salsa, chips, and Mexican red rice. The desserts of Churros (Mexican-style donuts with cinnamon and sugar) and Paletas (Mexican ice popsicles) returned me to childhood.

"What are we celebrating?" I asked, apropos of nothing.

"Jorge's business success," Aimee happily blurted, a remark which gained his warning look.

Chapter 138

Despite the exceptional food our party's mood went downhill after her remark. The light tone became banal: talk of a dumb Netflix series, and how a media sensation's nearly nude dress backfired badly.

"One can never tell if a plan will work," I said.

Though a well-worn sentiment my comment seemed to depress our party further and it broke up a little before nine.

Jorge and Aimee left in an Uber and I chose to walk the short distance home. A block from the restaurant a tall, heavy-set man approached and I instinctively braced and reached for my pistol.

"You won't need that. The Commissioner wants to see you," he said quickly.

Once in the Commissioner's car I wondered at our destination of a Wall Street apartment near Police Plaza, Why not meet as we had in a hole-in-the-wall restaurant, then told myself that he knew best.

Even before the COVID pandemic this financial hub had begun changing into housing for the newly rich. The apartment was tiny, about fourteen by sixteen feet though likely having a rent in the stratosphere. Asking it would have been impolite though my taxes were paying for it. After offering me coffee which I refused, the Commissioner immediately came to the point.

"The kidnapped girl's parents insisted on paying the ransom and the child was returned safely," he said.

"That's good news," I said.

"Not all of it. The note pinned to her jacket said, "Now that you know we keep our agreements, our next price will be greater."

"Greater," I repeated.

"Greater, and the victim may not be a single child. Consider public reaction if they threaten a school bombing or actually kidnap a high-ranking politician. We must get them first. What more have you learned about Jorge?"

"Only that he recently made a big score, and that Aimee knows of it," I said.

Chapter 139

"Do you consider her directly involved?" the Commissioner immediately asked, responding to my changed expression.

"I hope not," I said, looking down.

"Don't blame yourself. What happens isn't your responsibility. She'll have made her grave or not," he said, and I winced at his phrasing.

"Come! You're coming home with me," he insisted. "And it's not *that* though I'd take it as a compliment if you thought it might be. You need a mother tonight and my wife's the best. I'll say you're an officer who's had a big shock and needs respite, which is true. She cherishes the role ever since our kids left home."

Interpreting my weak smile as assent, he steered me back to the car where his driver waited.

"Home," the Commissioner directed.

Surprisingly, his home was located in the Bronx within a mile of my grandmother. Large and within a private leafy gated community, it had a scenic view and suburban feel.

"Here you don't need a car. We have shuttle buses to the Metro-North Railroad and express buses to Manhattan's East and West Side," his wife informed me as she proudly showed me around the house.

Her feeling was understandable since it was a homemaker's dream having great flow and ample room for entertaining with sliding glass doors opening to the rear patio and large dining deck. The center-island kitchen had a quartz countertop, peninsula breakfast bar, and stainless-steel Bosch appliances. The house had six bedrooms, seven bathrooms, and a private office for her husband.

"We needed the space for our four kids and grandchildren when they visit. Now I don't want to hear anything about your trouble. You're here to relax," she said, with a certainty that reminded me of my grandmother.

So I did.

Chapter 140

My respite took more than one evening. At the insistence of the Commissioner's wife, Helen, and without resistance from me, I spent the next two days at their home which she insisted I consider as mine. The office survived without me, Tilden phoning once for an update and reassurance, and Aimee doing her own thing. I phoned my grandmother to tell her I was well and was staying with friends in the Bronx and would soon visit. Having lived within my mind for so long, I had only recently begun to recognize my need for others.

I slowly became another of Helen's children and sank back into childhood. Doctor Hess might have termed this regression but I viewed it as gaining what I never had: a real mother.

A mental splitting seemed to occur as my identities separated: a child with parents who did all for them but also a battler against evil. Late one evening, after Helen went to bed, I shared my fear of failure with the Commissioner.

"I'm not worried. You're Joe's daughter. He was a survivor and so are you. I'll tell you a story about him. Once, while being driven to be murdered by criminals who feared that he'd doubled on them, he sat with bound hands beside the driver with another heavy in back.

"Through their search for his gun, they ignored what looked like a pen but contained a knife. During the drive he first cut himself free and then the throat of the driver before killing the other. You'll do fine too."

"My father was a good man," I said tremulously.

"Yes, and even more of a hero by those knowing the whole truth," he said.

I was left to wonder what that was since the Commissioner then sent me to bed.

Chapter 141

"So, are you dating anyone?" my grandmother asked upon my arrival home.

"Not seriously. Work takes all my time," I said.

"All work and no play..." she opined the ancient saying.

I smiled but didn't argue. It felt good being home and not having more to consider than washing one's hair, a situation which I knew wouldn't last. Vacations were intended to fortify for the next battle, or so my father theorized since he never took them. How could he relax when facing so many enemies I thought, which was also as my life seemed to be becoming.

After arriving in the office, the structure of legal practice resumed as depositions began. A deposition is a witness' sworn out-of-court testimony that is used to gather information. It is part of the discovery process and may be referenced at trial. The witness being deposed is called the "deponent."

Those present during a deposition are the deponent, the attorneys for interested parties, and a person qualified to administer oaths. Depositions are recorded electronically and all parties may question the witness. Lawyers are forbidden to coach their client's testimony, and the lawyers' ability to object to questions is limited.

Because depositions are hearsay they are inadmissible at trial except when a party admits something which is against their interest, when a witness' testimony at trial contradicts their deposition, and when a witness is unavailable at trial.

The first witness to be deposed was the psychiatrist who cleared the youth for discharge before he murdered. I felt no sympathy for the doctor as he sweated in the proverbial hotseat. "A doctor doesn't have the *right* to make a mistake," my law school professor raged, despite having earned his fortune from their errors.

"Thank you for taking the time from your busy schedule to be with us today," I said, beginning my questioning.

My professors also insisted that winning lawyers are courteous.

"What professional instruments did you use in your evaluation before recommending release of the boy who thereupon murdered my client's wife?" I asked.

Chapter 142

The psychiatrist wavered. We both knew that an evasive answer was needed since his accurate answer was likely "none."

"No formal testing was conducted, apart from my twenty-three years of professional expertise," Doctor Muller replied.

"Did you consider using psychological testing to determine the youth's mental state before his discharge?" I pressed.

"No."

"Why not?"

"Because such testing is the expertise of psychologists, all of whom lack medical training," he said officiously.

"So you consider their findings irrelevant to formulating a mental health diagnosis?" I asked.

"Not irrelevant but complementary, secondary to the psychiatrist's evaluation."

I looked down at papers, as if considering my next question though already knowing it.

"Please describe your professional training," I asked.

Doctor Muller responded confidently to this expected question. Now we were on his turf.

"I possess a medical degree from New York University Medical School where I also completed my psychiatry residency.."

"Were you ever rejected for training for which you applied?" I asked.

This question was *not* usual.

"One always apples to more institutions than where they're admitted, just as a high school seniors may apply to twenty colleges but only attend one," he said, his nervous smile sensing where I might be going.

"We're speaking of trained psychiatrists, not high school seniors,." I said brusquely.

"Yes."

"Have you ever applied for training to become a psychoanalyst?" I asked.

"Yes," he said, shifting uneasily in the chair.

"How many institutions did you apply to?" I asked.

"Two."

"Did you complete such training?"

"No."

"Why not?"

"I wasn't admitted to either program."

"You weren't admitted to either program," I repeated emphatically. "Why was that?"

"Who can say. Admission criteria vary and they might have wanted more women candidates that year," he said with a smile.

"So you weren't admitted because of prejudice against men?" I asked.

"I didn't say that."

"I'm sorry. I'll rephrase my question. Was psychological testing used to determine suitability for that training?" I asked.

When he didn't respond I asked, "Do you need me to repeat the question?"

"No. Yes, psychological testing was used by both institutions."

"Do you recall which tests were used?" I asked.

"The Rorschach Psychodiagnostics Test and the Thematic Apperception Test."

"Which were administered by psychologists?" I asked, though knowing the answer.

"Yes."

"Did you fail those tests?"

"I never learned the results."

"For how long have these tests been used in psychiatric practice?" I asked.

"The Rorschach Test since the 1920s and the Thematic Apperception Test since the 1930s."

"A very long time," I said.

"Yes."

"And have they not been considered the 'gold standard' for personality assessment"? I asked.

"Doctor Muller?" I asked after his lengthy silence.

"They have been so described," he said.

"Yet when deciding whether to release a potentially homicidal youth you failed to have him so tested despite having *two* psychologists on staff," I said.

"I have no further questions," I said after his lengthy silence.

Chapter 143

The next witness to be deposed was Albert, the last roommate of the accused murderer, Jasper.

"How long were you been a resident of the institution?" I asked.

"For nine months," Albert replied nervously.

"And for how long did you share a room with Jasper?"

"Two months. He didn't get along with his other roommate."

"How do you know that?"

"Because he told me."

"What did he say?"

Albert hesitated before replying.

"You must reply truthfully. You're under oath," I reminded.

"Okay. Well he said his roommate was a douchebag and he'd had to punch him out," Albert said.

"He 'punched him out,'" I repeated.

"Yes."

"That was four months before he committed the murder," I said.

"Yes I guess," Albert said.

"Did you get along Jasper?" I asked.

"Well enough. He never punched me," Albert said.

The opposing lawyer grimaced and I repressed a smile.

"During the time that you shared a room with Jasper, did he say anything about his plans when leaving the institution?" I asked.

"You mean talking about killing someone?"

"Any plan," I said.

"No, he was closemouthed except what he said about the staff."

"What did he say about them?" I asked.

"Well, he liked the English and music teachers but said the psychiatrist was a douchebag. He used the word a lot," Albert said apologetically.

"Did he say why he felt that?" I asked.

"Because he didn't listen to him. During sessions he would talk on the phone to his girlfriend and stockbroker and sometimes seemed to doze off. Jasper thought he might've been on drugs."

"During Jasper's therapy sessions his doctor spoke on the phone with his girlfriend and stockbroker and almost dozed off?" I asked.

"That's what he said. that Doc Muller was a douchebag."

With this, the opposing counsel suggested we take a break and I didn't object.

Chapter 144

Albert's testimony did it. Twenty-minutes later the issue of settlement was raised. "Without admitting fault on their part and so the plaintiff wouldn't suffer further during trial," the opposing counsel said

We both smiled, knowing this boilerplate statement to be total bullshit. It was money that really mattered. The testimony demolished their case and a jury would undoubtedly award far more than we settled for.

They offered ten-million-dollars, to compensate for the husband's suffering and loss of his wife's income. I presented this offer to Tilden together with my law-school derived opinion that the initial offer was merely a place to start. He instructed me to follow my judgment and I did.

In my next meeting with the institution's attorney I said that my client had scoffed at their offer but would consider thirty-five-million-dollars. The attorney rolled his eyes, I rolled mine, and we agreed on twenty-five-million dollars. We shook hands, informed the judge of settlement, and parted as friends. He told me, in confidence, that he had been authorized to offer up to thirty-five-million-dollars to settle.

"Win some, lose some," I said with a smile.

Our firm's fee agreement with Tilden was for thirty-percent of the award less expenses. But, perhaps from childhood instilled Catholic guilt, I recoiled at accepting so much money for so little professional time. Our fee would be three-million-dollars, I told Tilden.

"I'm grateful as will my daughter when she's older but are you sure?" he asked.

"Absolutely, and may you both be blessed with future happiness," I said, accepting his hug and kiss on the cheek. A minute later I thought what Doctor Hess would have said, "You're making amends for your father."

Chapter 145

Aimee was unhappy with my decision since it reduced her earnings too.

"Thirty-percent of the settlement is what Tilden agreed to and what every lawyer would take. He'd have gotten nothing if it weren't for our work. Are you crazy?" she said angrily.

Since she'd spent most workdays shopping leaving me to do the work, I felt miffed by her criticism but let it go. A law partnership is a marriage in which you must choose your battles, was another axiom I'd learned.

"Okay, since we didn't discuss it you'll get two-thirds of the fee instead of half," I said, with as much smile as I could muster.

"Done!" Aimee exclaimed. Instantly leaving the office with a smile, maybe to get another tattoo or piercing I thought nastily.

Another thought of my father arose, his depiction of tattoos and piercings as "abominations" and "low-class," warning me against getting any which I never did. This had been the second thought from childhood in as many hours. "You never leave the past behind," Doctor Hess had said during our first session.

News of my legal victory spread through the office and staff dropped in to congratulate me with Hamilton's offer of a job further brightening my mood. Feeling that I deserved a break, I left to go window-shopping along Madison Avenue's elegant displays. I had just reached Sixty-Eighth Street when I received a phone call from Aimee.

"I need you," she said hoarsely.

"What's wrong?" I asked.

"Please come, I'm home," she begged.

"Coming!" I said, and hailed a taxi.

My respite was over.

Chapter 146

When thinking of Aimee my memory often returns to our first meeting at school, fearing recognition as she sat beside me. As I stared at her facial piercings she unashamedly named them.

"The curved barbell on my upper lip is called a Jestrum. The one on my lower lip is called an Ashley. The one through my nose is called a Nasallang. It joins three piercings through the septum and nostrils."

"Do you have more?" I couldn't help asking.

"I can't show you here. Maybe later," she said slyly.

I forced a smile while remembering my father's admonition: "Piercing is an outlet for girls seeking attention to make up for their lack of purpose in life."

"Don't look so shocked. Earrings are piercings too though you don't wear them," she noted.

"I gave up after it got infected and healed crooked beneath the surface. Makes it hard to find the back of the piercings, and wearing heavy earrings hurt a lot too."

This exchange began our friendship despite having markedly different backgrounds. Her father was a hedge fund manager with inherited wealth and her mother was what in earlier times had been termed a socialite, spending her time organizing charity events to get herself noticed.

Aimee grew up on her own, at a variety of American and European boarding schools where she learned secrecy, seduction, and drug use. Her freckled, easily smiling face was American Mid-West while mine was of dour Swede.

"What happened?" I asked, when I arrived at her apartment, though her bruised face and shuffling gait made it obvious.

Chapter 147

Aimee had regained composure from her frantic tone minutes earlier. She stood alone in the apartment which was neat. Not the movie version of a domestic battle, I noted.

"Jorge happened," she said with a hurt smile.

I waited for more, knowing that the details of such behavior are revealed slowly with embarrassment.

She sat, I sat, and we looked at each other.

"Maybe it was good I didn't have your pistol," Aimee said.

"You look like it was bad," I said.

"Jorge has a temper. He loses control."

I said nothing since condemning him would have accomplished nothing. Love is tunnel vision and Aimee was blinded. Maybe by his money and Maserati, maybe by his good lucks. I might have fallen for him too.

"What set it off?" I asked though sensing what it was, remembering his flash of rage when Aimee mentioned his "big score" during our dinner.

"My being quiet tends to bother him but so does talking too much. He's lately been uptight and living with him is like walking on eggshells."

The advice, to "drop him," hung on my lips but I restrained myself. She wouldn't have listened, just felt that I didn't understand, damaging our friendship and my ability to monitor Jorge. Who, not she, was my real interest.

Though both Aimee and I were the product of imperfect childhoods, our friendship would not ordinarily have taken root since we were too different. Despite its lacks, she'd had a conventional family while I was a product of film-noir.

"Where's Jorge now?" I asked, seeking useful information.

"Out with friends. They'll be back soon."

"Do you want me to leave?" I asked.

"No, stay. You'll be a calming influence and he likes you."

I wasn't sure how to take her statement. She'd always been sexually freer than me and I hoped he didn't have a threesome in mind.

Chapter 148

We spent the next two hours cleaning her apartment. She was messy and I the opposite, neither having changed since school. Scrubbing bathtub grime hadn't been my expectation for a visit but I felt for her like a mother hen feels for their hobbling chick. A troubled childhood leaves marks and I had survived mine better, lacking her piercings except to my heart.

Had her increased sexual freedom enabled more fun? Without doubt but greater maturity counted too and I would never have involved myself with someone like Jorge no matter what my financial state.

Thoughts like these whirled as I focused on the tub's mold. Hadn't it ever been cleaned? I wondered, as I heard the commotion of Jorge's arrival.

Nattily dressed, he embraced Aimee who winced as he kissed her injured face. Then he noticed me watching, scrub-brush and Clorox Plus Tilex Mold and Mildew Remover in hand.

"I hope that's not intended for me," he said with a smile.

"That depends," I said coldly, before reminding myself why I was there and being unable to think of a clever innocent retort.

"I shouldn't have, darling," he said to Aimee before addressing me. "I've had a temper since my fucked-up childhood. Striking out when someone upsets me rather than asking what's really bothering me despite knowing that anger accomplishes nothing," he said.

That's something Doctor Hess might have said, I thought before entering my role of understanding friend.

"Mine was fucked-up too. I absolutely understand," I said vehemently.

Despite the disappointment in Aimee's expression I felt satisfaction since Jorge's smile showed that he'd bought my line.

Remembering what I held, I said, "I'll get rid of these," and returned to the bathroom.

Chapter 149

I left a half-hour later. Stress from playacting contented friend was increasing and "It was a long day," I said.

"Aimee told me the legal victory. I couldn't be prouder of you both," Jorge said, tightening his hug of Aimee who attempted a smile.

While walking to the door I felt as if I were leaving a funeral. At least it's not your's, I thought pessimistically. But the early bedtime that I'd intended wasn't to be. Minutes later I received a call on my burner phone from the Commissioner. "I'll be outside your apartment building," he said abruptly and disconnected.

After entering his car it sped to a deserted street on the far west side of Manhattan.

"Report," the Commissioner said angrily when the car stopped.

Being certain that he didn't mean my legal work, I told him of Aimee's frantic call and Jorge's later arrival from clubbing.

"What did Jorge ask?" the Commissioner asked, explaining when I seemed confused.

"You can learn from a person's questions what they want to know, what they hope and fear, and what tricks they're up to," he said.

"He didn't ask anything, just pretended to be ashamed of hitting Aimee earlier. Which he blamed on his lousy childhood despite knowing that behaving impulsively is a mistake. I pretended sympathy."

"It's good you did. We've been watching him and his associates. He must have noted and we have video of what happened."

He paused and I suddenly didn't want to learn.

"One of his friends walked to our agent's car and knocked on the closed window. When it opened he killed him with a silenced pistol, then stood waving his hand as if he were arguing with him to deceive passersby. Only an experienced gunman can do that."

Silence descended until I volunteered my embarrassing thought.

"Aren't you afraid that I'll *like* Jorge and start working with you both?" I asked.

"No, for once you've chosen you can no longer be on both sides," the Commissioner said.

Chapter 150

"Things must be heating up," I said.

"Why do you think that?" the Commissioner asked.

"Because they otherwise wouldn't have risked so public a killing," I said.

"Or they're raising the flag, warning to take them seriously," he said, and I sensed he was right.

"So what do we, what should I do?" I asked.

"There's no change in your assignment. Remain close to them, learning what you can while staying calm. An overly anxious agent is of no use and unlikely to survive a tight spot."

"So I should keep my gun handy?" I asked rhetorically.

"Always."

It had been a long ride for so brief a conversation but taking such precaution was wise. We didn't know how large Jorge's group was or even whether he headed it or was a hired hand. To avoid being seen they dropped me off at a coffee-shop favored by taxi-drivers. Before hiring one, I sat alone nursing a large orange juice, a frightened stranger involved in a world I never made.

That night's sleep lifted my spirits and cleared my mind to consider our conversation. Though uneasy, I hadn't objected to the Commissioner's comment: "I'm not a puppet-master. The most I do is to lead someone along the chosen path they're destined to follow."

But was this true? I asked myself. Had he recruited me *both* from opportunity and my heritage, being the child of an assassin for a potentially needed duty. A sobering thought which Doctor Hess couldn't help me with.

Well, if so there's no better time for love I thought, in a line that must have been borrowed from a romance novel I read. But people read for advice too, don't they?

Chapter 151

Despite my lengthy education, I've hadn't been sure what loving someone meant. Was it being unable to concentrate on anything until their arrival or an emptiness aroused by their thought. So, like the avid student I'd always been, I suddenly determined to study love. And, by chance, a suitable research subject arrived.

Brian is two years older than me. His father was the lawyer who'd gained me court approval to be present during the execution and Brian was a hanger-on in his father's office during our meetings. Both being instinctive loners, we gravitated toward each other, encouraged by adults who recognized my fragility.

Despite the headline-grabbing events, Brian and I had played as children do. His preference for Chess and mine for Chutes And Ladders, a babyish game which Doctor Hess might have interpreted as indicating my need to regress.

Though our periods on Columbia University's campus matched for several years during college and law school, we had barely spoken, just waved when noting the other. He perhaps thinking that I'd preferred to forget the earlier years or not knowing how to relate to this grown female, one so unlike the childish image of his memory.

Yet the ease with which we spoke at our meeting years later could have derived from the setting: a Yoga class sponsored by the Bar Association having the goal of fostering a lawyer's calm and inner peace.

"Don't we know each other?" Brian asked in a far more relaxed tone than I remembered from years before.

What a great Yoga instructor, I thought, for the class had barely begun!

Chapter 152

The instructor was a tall, slim, woman in her forties, Madame Freya. That she was also an attorney confirmed her expertise in our eyes despite her surprising introductory remarks.

"Yoga is often viewed as a sexy-feeling activity taught by sexually magnetic people though I won't ask for a show of hands about me. Some *may* be here because they heard that practicing yoga improves one's sex life though that's not what it ever promised, its history being as anti-sex as it can get.

"An ancient yoga concept called *bramacharya* is loosely translated as celibacy. Another translation is *sexual continence* which sounds just as disgusting."

Her smile reduced the embarrassment of those who tittered.

"To stem the landslide of those preparing to leave, I want to assure you this isn't true. Regardless of interpretation, yoga *can* improve your sex life by allowing you to be more confident and relaxed in your body. When practiced consistently and well you'll be more attuned to the needs and feelings of others, which makes you a better sex partner. So it might *not* be accidental that our ratio of males to females is about even," she said with a smile.

A few looked about the room mentally counting but most stared fixedly toward the instructor.

"To sum up, yoga will improve your sex life by making you *less* interested in sex."

Though lawyers are trained to argue both sides of a dispute, her statement seemed ridiculous, causing some to look about the room as if thinking there might be something better to do that evening.

"Let me tell you a story. When I was younger there were times I had more sex than now and sometimes less. Either way, everything seemed in pursuit of sex. I stayed out later than I should, left lengthy telephone messages and said dopy things to the men I stared at. My problem wasn't having sexual desire. which is a basic human want, but letting it control my life. Misunderstandings and unhappiness arose because my mind was clouded by sex.

"My early years of yoga practice didn't help, it being in hot-bod Los Angeles where sex is everywhere. What yoga teaches you is not to ignore your sexual urges but to observe them. Not that sex leads to suffering but that our attachment to it can. When the mind gets greedy the body gets weird and can drive one mad. I learned to acknowledge these thoughts and then let them go, seeking contentment when they both arise and dissipate. Then, when it's time to have sex, I'm content.

"Having heard this, if anyone wants to leave I'll refund your fee. Does anyone?"

Her confidence was justified by the hooting and clapping that followed.

Chapter 153

I've read of yoga instructors whose exercises cause pain and worse but Madame Freya's didn't. Afterward I felt relaxed and energized, with anxieties vanished.

"Calming, isn't it," Brian said as he rose from the floor.

"Almost as good as sex," I blurted.

I felt my face redden and wondered what got into me. Was it the instructor's description of how yoga improved her sex life?

Brian stared for a moment but didn't respond, making me grateful. It would have been awkward if he'd suggested a hotel room rather than the Starbucks downstairs, to which I instantly agreed.

"So how's your career going?" he asked once we were seated.

"Very well," I said, and described my recent victory.

"I'd say spectacularly. To get a huge settlement that quickly shows talent," Brian said.

"Maybe more luck than talent. Napoleon wrote that he wanted lucky generals, not smart ones," I said.

"And modesty," Brian said.

"Thank you. How's your work going?" I asked.

"The usual for a junior at an ancient law firm. The job market isn't great and I accepted a position at my father's law firm after his funeral. He'd been its standard-bearer," Brian said.

"I'm sorry, I hadn't heard. What happened?" I asked.

"A homeless nutcase knifed him on Park Avenue, in a robbery gone wrong or just being in the wrong place," Brian said.

"He was a great lawyer and a good man, a father to me during..."

"When we played together," Brian said.

"You were my only friend," I said.

Silence hung heavy as we lingered in memories.

"I'd better get going," I said.

"I'll walk you home," he said.

"Come upstairs. I want you to see the letter your father sent me after the execution," I said.

But that was for later. A moment after he entered my apartment, I threw my arms around his neck and thrust my tongue into his mouth.

Chapter 154

Brian didn't seem surprised. Thankfully, since I don't know what I would have said if he asked what I was doing. But if my perception had been that wrong the greater worry would have been my sanity. The next moments seemed natural, as if they'd been written in the stars when we were children. Which is what I said and he agreed.

"We were never only friends. I sensed this when you were fourteen but felt you were too young to hear," he said.

"I was and would have been too scared. My world was crashing and I wouldn't have been able to cope with that too.. Sex was something I'd read about and for grownups which I wasn't."

"I never could imagine how you survived that time," Brian said.

"Nor can I. I lived one day at a time, behaved properly, and let myself be led by others," I said.

"Was it only your decision to witness the execution??"

Though being an odd question to ask as we lay naked, it was understandable. Brian wanted to know me intimately, and for this I was grateful.

"During those days things rolled through my mind like stones on a road, all politeness but feeling nothing. The decision was mine, possibly encouraged by a novel I read about Thomas Cromwell, Henry VIII's brutal fixer of Anne Boleyn's execution because she didn't bear him a child. I still remember its poem:

'Bluff King Hal was full of beans,
He married half a dozen queens.
Anne Boleyn was his second wife,
He swore to cherish her all his life,
But seeing a third he wished instead,
He chopped off poor Anne Boleyn's head.'

Dead To Life

"Or it might have been the delusion that my father would be saved by my presence, that a father *couldn't be executed* within sight of his child. I wasn't thinking rationally."

Brian hugged me since the moment didn't permit words, my experiences evidencing that the veneer of civilization can be brittle.

Chapter 155

Without thinking, our relationship adopted the comfort of earlier years with the added joy of sex. But as Madame Freya had advised, sex didn't consume but was our gift for sharing. Both being lawyers, work complemented our relationship for we understood its stresses and valued insider anecdotes. One about loneliness I particularly related to.

"A former partner came to the office yesterday, desperate for conviviality. Having achieved his lifelong goal of judge both pleased and distressed him," Brian said..

"'I didn't realize how lonely a judge's life is,' he said. At the health club, clad in T-shirt and shorts, he'd passed friends who said only, 'Good morning, your honor,' repeating this as he returned from the rowing machine.

"He said there was an instant isolation after gaining office, like being quarantined. Routine activities became awkward with friendships distorted and new contacts inhibited as lawyers bowed and scraped, laughing at his lamest jokes. He said those who never bothered greeting him in the past now praised the wisdom of his decisions, but that he has enough self-awareness to realize they were groveling at the robe and not his intellect, with his name being repeated incessantly from the belief that people most appreciate its sound.

"To avoid partisan advantage he's been forced to devise rules about which invitation to accept and weigh every word as to how much he can say and on what subject and to whom. Trusted friends are valued with new ones harder to make. He said he can't go three miles over the speed limit or curse or drink too much, fearing trouble from the smallest stumble."

"Did you ask if he felt the job was worth it?" I asked.

"I did and he said it was the best legal job there is. That private practice lawyers measure success by beating the other side but as a judge his goal is simply to do justice, to render what's right."

Which is why I'm working with the Police Commissioner, I thought, but couldn't say. A secret remains secret only if unspoken had been another of my father's lessons.

Chapter 156

Years later I was to consider the week that followed as our honeymoon. There were no calls from the Commissioner but another with thanks from Tilden. I referred all potential clients except for a pro bono case which stirred my interest. Which Aimee grudgingly accepted after I said it would gain us the needed provision of fifty hours of free legal services provided each year under Rule 6.1 of New York State's Rules of Professional Conduct. Passing the Bar Exam was hard and losing her license would be unacceptable.

I didn't express my nasty thought that getting a new tattoo might reduce her anguish, later realizing that having it could indicate that our already shaky partnership was nearing its end.

The no-fee case involved a father imprisoned for murdering his wife. Their nine-year-old daughter had witnessed the crime and her testimony led to his conviction. He now sought visitation with her in prison, a demand to which both the girl's therapist and Child Protective Services witnesses objected. And, as these things go, the father had his lawyer and the girl had me.

Her father had been a notorious drug dealer and the courthouse was ringed with police, there being rumor that his gang would try to free him but nothing happened. After attorneys did their part, my victory aroused praise though it was really the girl who won.

"What was your thought after the verdict?" Brian had asked.

I hesitated before answering, having read that a woman shouldn't tell a man too early that she loves him but also feeling the time was right.

"My first thought was that I saved the girl's life. My second was that I want your baby," I said.

Chapter 157

I didn't know how Brian would respond. A child creates responsibilities, which not all men want no matter how much they value their girlfriend. But I needn't have worried. His response to my words was an embrace and question: "Only one?" These honeymoon moments were interrupted by the shrill of the burner phone given me by the Commissioner.

"Must you take it?" Brian asked.

"I'm sorry, I must," I said.

My leaving the room to answer the phone raised alarm since this behavior is popularly thought to evidence an affair. Allaying this suspicion without explanation is something that even the most talented lawyer would flub, I thought.

"My car will be downstairs in ten minutes," the Commissioner said and hung up.

I must give Brian a *really good* explanation, I thought.

"I have to go," I said, upon re-entering the bedroom. Then, before he could respond, I said in a deadly serious tone, "I vow on my father's grave that it's work and not another man."

"An emergency?" he asked rhetorically.

"Yes and I can't explain now but will soon," I said.

I automatically pat my holster-vest to check for my pistol and Brian started. He wasn't born yesterday.

"Is it dangerous?" he asked with evident concern.

"Maybe though not just now. But don't worry! I have allies and also vowed to bear your child."

"I'll try not to worry. When I do I'll remind myself that you're your father's daughter," he said, with a forced grin.

"In more ways than you could imagine," I said.

Thoughts of Brian remained in my mind as I entered the Commissioner's car.

"You look happy," he said.

"I am. I've decided to have a baby," I said in an even tone.

Momentarily speechless, he sputtered, "Not immediately I hope."

"No, I've heard that it takes nine months," I said cheekily.

"I could use good news," he said in a deliberate tone.

"What happened?" I asked.

Upon learning, I couldn't help wondering if it was fair bringing a child into this world.

Chapter 158

"'This is to provide you with evidence of our seriousness. Next time we'll do worse,' the note read. It was taped to the shirt of a thirteen-year-old, the daughter of a United States Senator," the Commissioner said.

Her photos were thrust into my face without asking. More than most I had learned the horrors of the world too soon.

"She was raped and the sides of her face were slashed, giving her a forced grin. Her nipples were cut off and a dildo shoved in her anus," the Commissioner said.

"Is she alive?" I asked.

"She's alive. Not wanting to live but she'll have the best medical treatment."

"What happened?" I asked.

"According to the housekeeper she went to a girl-friend's home two blocks away after school. She was found in an alley, bleeding and semi-conscious, by a passerby in early evening."

"Has she been questioned?" I asked.

"Gingerly as you'd expect. She only remembers being grabbed and having a pad forced against her mouth and nose before losing consciousness."

"At least she didn't feel the pain," I said.

"That's to come," the Commissioner said, and I nodded.

"You believe Jorge was involved?" I asked.

"Cutting off nipples is his motto. He was arrested as a teenager for rape and an identical assault. Released when the victim changed her story. The rumor was she was threatened and paid off."

"What can I do?" I asked.

"Stay close to them. Something'll turn up, maybe from Aimee."

"Stomaching him now won't be easy. Criminals like him deserve a bullet, not a trial," I said.

Dead To Life

"You're your father's daughter. Take care," the Commissioner said, and squeezed my hand.
"Always," I said.

Chapter 159

The Commissioner's car, which had been driven aimlessly as we spoke, dropped me off two blocks from my apartment. I didn't immediately return home, needing time to calm and ready myself for Brian's understandable questions. Lying wasn't an option but neither was telling him the truth. So I walked and tried to think of a third option, which didn't come.

To delay this confrontation, I seated myself in a small local park, a popular refuge in bustling mid-town, and sipped an orange juice bought at its kiosk. A girl of about five, seated on an adjoining bench, spoke to her doll. "I know the Alphabet Song. Let's sing it," and she did. "A B C D E F G, H I J K L M N O P, Q R S T U and V, W X and Y and Z. Now I know my ABCs. Next time, won't you sing with me."

The child turned to me. "Let's sing the Alphabet Song," she said. Her watching mother smiled permission and I sang the song with her daughter. "You're a good teacher," I told the child and she beamed.

"Do you have children?" her mother asked.

"Not yet but I'm hoping for one. That's what I told my boyfriend today," I said.

"Men are a different species," she said.

I laughed, then thought of the mutilated girl.

"I'm sorry. Your expression changed so much. I didn't mean to upset you," the woman said.

It isn't what you said. I just learned of a terrible crime toward a child making me wonder if it's right bringing a child into this world," I said.

"They're our hope for the future and our commitment to a better world," she said.

That moment, as we stared into each other's eyes, I thought we could be friends, which aren't easy to acquire as an adult. She'd apparently thought the same since she moved with her daughter to my bench, told me her name, and said she lived down the block. I then revealed my name despite fearing the frequent reaction which didn't happen. Maybe I've finally become anonymous I dared hope.

Chapter 160

Walking slowly didn't help me decide what to tell Brian when I arrived home. The doorman's greeting met my frozen smile and my elevator ride reminded me of a condemner's trip to the gallows. But I needn't have worried. Brian was reading as I entered the living room and his greeting was jovial.

"The nation is adopting your style," he said.

"Huh?" I replied, this being my lame response to puzzlement since childhood.

"Yes. A state legislature just authorized their judges to carry pistols under their robes because of the 'violent atmosphere touching upon the courtroom.'"

"Who could object?" I asked, feeling relief at this neutral topic.

"Some did. One legislator described our era as 'weird' and another said the proposal was 'Wild West revisited.' The bill passed with overwhelming support, putting you in the forefront of style."

"What motivated the bill?" I asked, extending the conversation on this impersonal subject.

"The report that a drug cartel had threatened a 'bloody retaliation campaign' against the entire law enforcement apparatus including judges. It noted that recent litigants have acted similarly with an increase in courtroom shootings from California to New York.

"Opposing legislators inveighed against the 'John Wayne attitude,' the idea that adding a gun to the courtroom would increase its security, adding that a judge might mistakenly shoot someone. They said a killer wouldn't approach them head-on like in an old Western but shoot them in the back. But it was another line that won the argument."

"What was it?" I asked.

"That judges should be as well armed as the people appearing before them."

"Now I've become *Jane Wayne*," I said, with a downcast look.

"Okay, what's wrong? You've looked gloomy since returning. I know I'm not a Romeo but was I *that* bad a lover?" he asked with mock horror.

I smiled, my worry disappeared, and I told him the truth. As much as it was safe to reveal. knowing that not only in movies does a man feel it is their duty to protect their woman.

Chapter 161

"I've had minimal sexual experience before you but couldn't imagine loving being better. I'll tell you what's happening but our lives depend on keeping it secret," I said.

"Are you *serious*?" Brian asked, with a shocked look.

"As serious as the grave that could be ours," I said.

"Okay," he said, and I began.

"I recently learned that my father was much more than his reputation. That he'd saved American lives while in the military and after being discharge was recruited for another campaign in which he performed heroically too."

As I continued, Brian's eyes nearly goggled.

"The City was once ruled by gangsters demanding kickbacks from restaurants, unions, and business owners. No building went up or restaurant meal sold without graft being paid. Nor was government safe. Building and restaurant inspectors who didn't follow orders had their car tires slashed followed by worse. Homes were firebombed and people murdered."

"Where was the law?" Brian asked.

"Prevented from acting by clever lawyers and legal constraint. A group of fed-up influential citizens decided to fight fire with fire, recruiting my father as the Spear of Justice as they termed him. He cleaned up the city by killing crime-lords and their henchmen, making it livable again."

"So why was he executed?" Brian asked.

"After being caught by police who weren't in the know, he took the fall for the others, a hero to the end for all of us," I said, and cried.

Brian held me until my sobbing subsided.

"That's long in the past. How would that endanger us now?" Brian asked.

"Some still hate my father. They once came after me but I was saved and warned to be careful. Then, without asking, I was issued a pistol permit and given recommendation for training. There've recently been horrible crimes with the threat of more if a huge ransom isn't paid. I was recruited to help in the investigation," I said.

"Why you? You're..."

"Yes, a woman," I interrupted.

"I didn't mean that."

"No, I know you didn't I'm just nervous. They chose me because I know Aimee, the girlfriend of the man they suspect," I said.

"How dangerous is your assignment?" Brian asked with an intent gaze.

"Not so much until what I was recently asked to do," I said.

Chapter 162

Silence hung heavy until Brian asked, "What do they want you to do?"

"Wear a bug during meetings and hide bugs in Aimee's apartment," I said, sighing.

"They must have pros to do it. Why you?" Brian asked.

"Her boyfriend's buddy stays there so they can't go in. I can, being a friend," I said.

"It's risky."

"Tell me again," I said resignedly.

"You can refuse."

"I really can't. They once saved my life and other lives are at risk."

"You're your father's daughter all right. Show me the bugs," he said.

I removed them from the attaché case that was given me.

"They're simplicity itself, to be concealed in a room where you want to listen to conversations. Each device holds an activated SIM card that automatically places a call when people talk nearby. Full access is given to the conversation with the device being controlled through text-message based demands. I thought to gift Aimee with a desk calculator, desk lamp, laptop and mouse, and a electric power strip to use them at home. All except the laptop contain audio transmitters," I said.

"Any others?" Brian asked.

"There's a bugged sex toy but I can't think where to place it," I said.

Now Brian erupted "Huh" and I said, "Joking."

"A sense of humor can get one through a lot but giving gifts doesn't sound dangerous. The bugs are tiny, less than a half-inch," Brian said admiringly.

"And beautiful in a way unless finding one gets me killed," I said.

Dead To Life

"I won't let that happen," Brian said.

I smiled at his words of devotion though knowing that in the world I had entered they were meaningless.

Chapter 163

Brian continued arguing against my involvement, too upset to drop the topic.

"Those trained for violence come from the military or mean streets of the ghetto. I admire your courage but what makes you think you can be a spy. Their using you, an untrained person, is crazy," he insisted.

"Maybe, but every bold successful action seemed crazy at its inception," I rejoined.

And that's where the arguing ended, we both knowing that for love to continue it's critical to know when to give up. Also, that the best way to win an argument is to not argue.

Both my roommates were out that night. April, my bodyguard, to an office meeting, and Ingrid being hostess for Leonardo's party. Now, being completely alone, the apartment felt fully our home and I a traditional hausfrau. Cooking dinner (baked salmon, rice, broccoli) and scowling dramatically at his hope of chocolate pudding pie, a childhood favorite dessert. Before enjoying the classic romantic movie he'd downloaded, *Notorious*.

"Hmm..." I noted as it ended.

"What?" he asked innocently.

"You're still trying to win the argument," I said, and his blush gave him away.

Notorious is a 1946 American spy film directed by the famed director Alfred Hitchcock. It tells of an American government agent (Devlin) who privately loves but must enlist Alicia, to infiltrate a group of escaped Nazis conducting atomic research in Brazil after World War II. Ordered to discover their secrets, she marries one of the Germans who is an old chum. Later, outed as an American spy, she is slowly poisoned before being rescued by Devlin.

"I'm already married and won't be a bigamist," I said jokingly.

"That's not my fear," Brian said.

Later, snuggled close in bed, I believed the matter closed in my mind until a nightmare told me it wasn't.

Chapter 164

In the dream I was running through a house, trying to escape from someone or something chasing me. Being unarmed, I instinctively sought a weapon but there was none to be seen. Then my father appeared, almost like a ghost, directing me to get my Swan Security Blanket which lay in the hidden cabinet. I did, clutched my Swan, and instantly awoke.

"What's wrong?" Brian asked, my twisted movements having awakened him.

"Nightmare," I mumbled.

"Forget it. Your analyst must have told you that a nightmare is just a bad dream," he said, dismissively.

"No, not that. I must go home in the morning," I said.

"Do you want me with you?" he asked.

"Not now, it'll be a short visit. Soon we'll stay with my grandma for a weekend," I said.

"Have Romeo drive you," he cautioned, and I agreed.

Early in my therapy Doctor Hess said that dreams are created by our unconscious and can be hard to interpret by oneself. Still, I tried for hours before giving up. Then, an hour later, its meaning became clear: that safety lay with my Swan Security Blanket, a childhood treasure.

Once, when very young, I watched my father open a hidden compartment beneath a floorboard. Noticing me, he asked if I had anything of value that I wanted kept safe and I instantly gave him the blanket. "If ever you're frightened, what's hidden here will keep you safe," he said in a serious tone.

"Dreams can't predict the future but *can* give helpful advice, created from what we already know," Doctor Hess also said.

So after schmoozing over lunch with my grandmother, I went to my father's room. There, by his long-unused bed, I lifted the scatter rug, pressed the indentation in the floor and removed the metal box beneath. Opening it, I wasn't surprised by its contents and my father's advice from the grave.

Chapter 165

Inside the box was a Ruger twenty-two caliber pistol, two large manila envelopes containing stacks of hundred-dollar bills, and a letter. All lay upon my neatly folded Swan Security Blanket. I read the letter with shaking hands.

"Dearest Annika,
"Having had enemies throughout my life, I made provision for your safety with friends but that you now read this letter must indicate your fear. The Ruger and cash can be life-saving. Use them well. You, my beautiful daughter, are my gift to the world.
"Your loving father."

Romeo was playing chess online in the living room while my grandmother napped.

"Did you find what you were looking for?" he asked, looking up from the screen.

"I didn't know what I'd find but it wasn't unexpected," I said.

"He loved you, *really* loved you, you do know," he said.

"Always!" I said.

"And I'll always be here for you too," he said, before quickly looking away.

Being aware of Romeo's difficulty with emotion, I downplayed the moment and said playfully, "And I for you if you ever need a lawyer."

"Are you ready to leave?" he asked, our awkward moment having passed.

"As soon as I say goodbye to grandma," I said.

"This is my home," he said, nodding forcefully and apropos of nothing.

I stood thinking. Though healthy, my grandmother was getting on in years. Where would Romeo live when she died? Our family and home had long been his. So, without further thought, I decided.

"You've always been part of our family and this is your home. When my grandmother passes and this house is mine, I will give it to you. This will always be your home and you will always be my guardian," I said.

"Thank you," he said.

This was only the second time that I saw tears in his eyes, the first being when he learned of my father's death.

Chapter 166

"You're carrying *two* guns," Brian noticed as we undressed for bed.

"One was my dad's. I picked it up at home," I said.

"For luck, I guess. Is it registered?" he asked and I shrugged.

"Just be careful," he said, eyeing me closely.

I nodded and reflected that in recent days I had twice been told this.

Over the following days, I was frantically busy at work. Having been a casual worker, Aimee now left me to do nearly all the work despite sharing its income. Fashion and shopping were her current passions and she strove to become expert, the waiting room becoming depository for her discarded issues of *W* and *Darling* and *Harper's Bazaar*. She occasionally dropped not-so-subtle criticisms of my clothes which I ignored.

But I understood what was going on. Aimee wasn't naturally lazy but her relationship with Jorge had become more problematic than usual. He demanded that his girlfriend be a sounding board, acceding to his demands and his anger too.

"What's that?" I asked one day, indicating a bruise on her throat.

"It's nothing, just Jorge being a little too affectionate," Aimee said looking embarrassed.

"That doesn't look like a hickey to me," I said, angrily.

"Oh you know Jorge," Aimee said.

Yes, I think I do, I thought.

"I gave you a key to my apartment didn't I?" she asked.

"It's on my key ring," I said, pulling it from my purse and showing it.

"Just wanted to check. I've gotten forgetful and don't want to be locked out," she said.

"Doesn't Roberto practically live there?" I asked.

"He uses hard drugs. Can be dead to the world and isn't always friendly when he wakes up," Aimee said with a hint of embarrassment.

Roberto was huge. At six-foot-five and three-hundred pounds, he'd worked as bouncer in a Juarez bar. His favored stories, told with relish, were of beatings that he'd given to problem customers.

"Be careful," I told Aimee, using what had become almost a cliché in my life

She smiled weakly.

Chapter 167

The next morning, a potential client had just entered my office when my cell phone rang. Grabbing it distractedly I heard Aimee's strangled voice.

"Annika.." she mumbled.

"I'm busy. Can I call you later?" I asked hurriedly.

But she just said my name.

"Are you alright?" I asked slowly and motioned for the client to sit.

My worry increased as she repeated my name and I heard what sounded like the phone dropping.

"I must leave, an emergency. Reschedule with my secretary," I blurted and rushed from the office with thoughts cascading through my mind: the mark on Aimee's neck, my nightmare, my father's pistol and farewell letter.

Lucking into a cruising taxi, I told the driver Aimee's address, adding, "It's an emergency. A hundred-dollars for getting me there fastest." He did and ten-minutes later I was opening her apartment's door, thankful for the spare key she'd given me.

The apartment's silence had caused me to think my fear was unwarranted but that was before I found Aimee. She lay unconscious on the floor with a clown-like smile on her face. This is caused by slashes like in the other attack, I told myself, as Jorge walked into the room holding a kitchen knife. Without thinking I pulled my father's pistol from its holster and covered him with it.

"What happened?" I asked, despite it being obvious.

"She talks too much and needed discipline. I'm about to pretty her nipples," he said calmly, as if we were discussing the weather.

"Like with the girl," I said.

"With her it was business. You understand."

I did, and the silence between us grew.

"How much will it cost for you to leave without calling the police?" he asked.

"You're negotiating?" I asked.

"People are always negotiating," he said, which is true.

"I'm a lawyer," I said, as if considering my price.

"So I'll be paying more than if you were a maid. Consider! If arrested, a high-priced psychiatrist will certify me mentally ill and a judge will hospitalize me until sane, if friends don't break me out of the hospital of course. Or maybe Aimee will be persuaded to testify she slashed herself in a drug-induced mania. You're a lawyer. You know how the justice system works," Jorge said.

It might have been his certainty or smile that determined my behavior but I never regretted it.

"Yes, I am a lawyer and do know. But there is a justice of the lawyer and the courtroom, and a justice of the Prophets and of God," I said slowly.

His smile had been changing into uncertainty when I shot him, center-mass as I had been taught. Then, walking closer, I shot him in the forehead, giving him a "double-tap" as I had also been instructed. After wiping my fingerprints from the gun and dropping it, I wiped everything that I'd touched in the apartment.

A block away, I seated myself on a bench in a crosswalk with cars speeding alongside. There, holding a crushed tissue over the receiver and feigning an accent, I phoned 911 and asked for an ambulance to be sent to Aimee's apartment. "A woman is dying," I said in a rushed voice.

After hanging up I cut the phone's SIM card with the nail scissor in my purse and dropped its pieces into a sewer grating before returning to my office. Praying that Aimee would survive, to be treated by the City's best plastic surgeon.

Chapter 168

"Did you manage your emergency okay?" the receptionist asked when I re-entered the office.

"Boyfriend trouble. You know how they can be," I said.

"I sure do!" she insisted and I forced a grin as she turned away to answer a call.

Once in my office I took off my shoes, lay on the sofa and ran the recent events through my mind, amazed at my calm. Am I *really* calm? I wondered. Then, determined to check, I reached for the small health kit in every office. Apart from antiseptic and bandages it contained a digital blood pressure monitor. Seating myself at my desk, I wrapped the cuff around my arm, pressed the button and read the truth seconds later. My blood pressure was perfect: one-hundred-twenty-two over seventy with a pulse rate of forty-nine. I really was okay!

The papers on the desk reminded me of work and I dug in. Working keeps dark thoughts away, my father had said. Surprisingly, Doctor Hess had advised this too.

The office phone's ring interrupted. "You have a call from a friend. He won't give his name," the receptionist said, and I told her to put the call through.

"Your burner seems not to work. I was concerned," the Commissioner said.

"I can't find it. Must have left it somewhere," I said casually.

"There've been developments," he said.

"Oh?" I said, innocently.

"An ambulance was called to Aimee's apartment. They found her slashed like the last victim and Jorge shot dead. His accomplice was asleep in another room, heavily drugged. She's at New York Presbyterian's Trauma Center. We don't know what happened. A gun on the floor is being checked for prints and to see if it's the murder weapon," he said.

"I'm not sorry about Jorge. He was a shit," I said.

"It's an assassin's gun like what your dad favored. You don't know anything about this do you?" he asked suspiciously.

"Only what you've told me. I must go to the hospital," I said in a rushed tone.

"Annika?"

"Yes."

"I was proud to be your father's friend and will always be yours."

Then, before I could respond, he hung up.

Chapter 169

Though conscious, Aimee's face was heavily bandaged and she looked a wreck.

"You're having a rough time," I said sympathetically.

"You might say that," she whispered hoarsely.

"Try not to worry. The firm is covering medical costs and will hire the best plastic surgeon. You'll look better!" I said with feigned brightness.

I sensed a smile under the bandages as Aimee held out a hand, pulling me close so my ear rested nearly on her mouth.

"The noise of the shots woke me for a moment and I saw. You saved my life," she said.

"That was a dream. It's best not to speak of it," I said softly.

"Never again," she promised.

I stayed with Aimee until the nurse arrived, then went looking for the doctor supervising her treatment.

"You seem short-staffed. I'd like a nurse to be with Aimee continually. She's a valued member of my firm which will cover all costs. You may know someone who wants private work," I said.

The doctor did and arrangements were made. Only then did I question this extravagance, thinking that it might reflect my feeling guilty at not having rescued her from Jorge earlier even if it likely wasn't possible. I was still obsessing this when I arrived home.

After telling Brian about Aimee's condition he remarked, "You're down to one gun."

"I think you should forget that," I said, in a severe tone.

He frowned but we never discussed the matter again.

I visited Aimee daily during the time she was in the hospital. When the police tape was removed from her apartment, I hired a company that specializes in cleaning crime scenes. They did a good job and even the closest inspection wouldn't reveal what happened there.

While taking Aimee home from the hospital I asked, "How did your interview with the police go?"

"It didn't take long since I know nothing, being unconscious when Jorge was killed. I didn't feel the need to have a lawyer present," she said in an innocent tone.

We both smiled.

Chapter 170

It's been three years since the events which paralyzed the City and captured headlines. My only phone calls with the Commissioner now are to extend invitations to dinner. He's become baby Josephine's favored courtesy uncle.

Brian and I named her after my father, Josephine for Joe, it being the closest equivalent though her looks, being Scandinavian, are mine. She is healthy and our joy.

Aimee too is well. Her plastic surgeon did superb work with her greatest temporary discomforts having been needing to keep her head elevated while lying down, using frequent cold compresses to reduce swelling, and avoiding activity. She was ordered to phone him her condition daily and report discomfort immediately. I noted his number for future reference and referral.

Work has been busy and, with this prosperity, we could afford our own office but chose to remain where we were. Habits are hard to change but we did insist on paying the current market rent.

Aimee changed after her surgery. Her shopping obsession disappeared, she works long hours, and removed her piercings. She had laser treatment to remove her tattoos but got a new one. It was to celebrate her survival and remind her to keep going no matter what happens. A winged bird with the words "STILL I RISE" underneath, it is on her butt where clients can't see it.

One evening, resting at home with Brian and Josephine toddling about us, I sensed that the saga which began on the day of my birth had ended. I was now free, free to love and free to be the mother I had lacked.

"We have a good life, don't we?" I murmured to Brian.

"The best, my darling, the very best," he said.

Dead To Life

www.ingramcontent.com/pod-product-compliance
Lightning Source LLC
Chambersburg PA
CBHW071852220626
47052CB00002B/83